CW01665985

The CryoShed
By
Sean E Robinson

To my father, Clive George Robinson.
Thanks for everything, the one and only Chez!

1

I'm literally freezing and can only see the tiny window, inches from my face, start to fog up because of the tiny blue light in the corner of the room. The condensation would be dripping on my forehead if it wasn't forming these geometric, sweeping crystallizing patterns. It's too tight in here to shiver, so I'm forcing myself to relax. The fear, actually, fear is a little strong, let's say, apprehension, is causing me to breathe quicker than normal. I need to calm down if this is going to work. The idea is that I freeze fast. By my calculations, I should be frozen through in about four hours. This will cause minimal damage to the cells in my body and the neurons in my brain.

When I wake up, I'm looking forward to a great many advances. Technological and philosophical outlooks towards the planet, science, religion and each other should be massively improved.

I'm betting on Artificial Intelligence being used to solve problems humans have been struggling with like; finding a cure for cancer, reversing global warming, feeding the hungry and preventing pandemics from shutting down the whole world. I especially look forward to robots being a part and parcel of everyday life. I've never had much luck dealing with people, so I think I'll get on quite well with robots. They'll be doing jobs that humans don't really want to do, and sex robots will be a totally acceptable part of society. No one will judge someone for wanting to use one. Personally, I'll feel right at home amongst programmable, semi-intelligent robots. I'm guessing that some people will want their robots to behave human-like and express strong emotions. I look forward to choosing out my own, one without too much back story programmed in. Extreme and unmanageable emotions are something I'm looking to get away from when I escape to the future. There's no way a robot will be as hard to figure out as a human girl. That's one thing I've learned this summer.

I'm from the year 2020, the shittest year in memory. I live in a place called Ashcave in Surrey. I imagine names will be classified differently in the future, making everywhere more part of the global community. But at the moment, the only thing connecting Ashcave to the global community is the Corona Virus. Where I live is suburban but yet somehow still cut off. I'm half an hour walk away from a train station, the nearest bus goes three stops and finishes at the hospital. The closest amenities to us is a parade of shops permanently locked in the 1970s. There's a butchers, a bakers, a hardware shop and a CoOp that sells most of what the three of the independent shops sell but worse quality. I had to walk or get a lift from my parents if I wanted to go anywhere. But I tended not to go anywhere, apart from school.

Ashcave is a place where I have nothing in common with anyone, apart from our proximity. I refused to succumb to the local small-minded way of thinking and be another sheep. I decided to transport myself to the future, where I know I will find more like-minded, forward-thinking, sensible people, like me. Of course, I know there are people in the world that have the same views as me right now and maybe one day if I studied and went to university, I'd get to meet some of them, create a bond, and maybe we'd even help the human race get back on track before the shit really hit the fan. But these were if, buts and a lot of maybes. I grew up on false promises and misdirected hopes. It only took me to my 15th birthday to realise I couldn't rely on the conventional ways of getting through life for me to get what I wanted. Without doing something drastic, taking some risks and thinking beyond that of a normal person, how could I escape my inferior friends, my constantly disappointing parents, boring test-driven school, Covid-19, air pollution, terrible music, reality TV and lad culture?
I, Patrick Waters, wasn't going to stand by and be miserable. So, I took action...

2

The first thing that comes to mind at the beginning of this story is the hellish situation I'm escaping from.

People will undoubtedly look back on the past with fondness, but I have very few pleasantries to reminisce about. People doubted themselves more than in any other time in history and turned that doubt into negativity aimed both inwards and outwards. For safety, they wanted to stay within their own little world, in their familiar towns and only be with people they knew, people with the same opinions, who dressed the same and, for some, even looked the same as well.

The alpha male was still king of this domain. Even though feminism and equal opportunities were spoken about a lot, I never really witnessed much of that being put into practice. The strong had power over the weak, and the stupid outgunned the intelligent. The senseless had something I couldn't compete with - outward self-confidence.

That brings me to my father, Del. The joke that is 'Del' can start with his name. His real name was David Waters (apparently, there is no doubt over him being my real dad, I've made inquiries in the past). He once scored a free kick in a football game about ten years ago, and his mates started calling him Del after the Italian free-kick specialist Del Piero. Instead of nick naming him after the more famous David Beckham, his mates went for a more obscure player who never even played in England. The nickname became worse when after a while, he started to introduce himself as Del. My mum even gave in and called him it occasionally.

Del was part of a social epidemic that was running wild at the time called Lad Culture. It basically meant that any time a man did anything, they could embellish the facts to their friends and then were called a 'Lad' because of it. Football, alcohol and casual sexism were the linchpins that kept lad culture glued together. It was everywhere, and I wanted nothing to do with it.

Among many other reasons, this was why I felt I had nothing in common with Del. I felt sorry for him to be honest. He constantly needed to impress his large group of male friends. Often upsetting my mum or me to gain laughs or 'lad points'. It was all just 'bants', though. Trust me. I knew all about banter. I learned it from him at 11 years old when he took a piss in my wellington boots before I went on a nature walk. Was it 'bants' when I set his passport on fire before a golf trip with 'the lads'? That was when I was quite young and naive. My plan for ruining his fun had worked and also completly backfired, meaning he was at the house, angry all week instead of being away. I never lowered myself to his level again after that.

Money and consumerism ran his life. Before Lockdown, he was out on the road as an insurance salesman. Sometimes gone for a few weeks at a time. I loved that. He couldn't resist giving me a small speech about being the man of the house while he was away. I was the man of the house when he was there, for Christ sake! He was a big child, never growing up, just continuing to get bigger as the years go on. Somehow, even though he was quite a large man, he always seemed to be in good shape. He played football twice a week and, as was customary where we lived, Cricket in the summer. He spoke about his games like he was a professional, and the papers reported on his form. All the goals he scored were 'epic' or 'just stroked in'. Listening to him talk about the games was the spoken word form of watching paint dry.

Having seen what women were attracted to in the 2020's I could understand what seduced my mother. He was an imbecile, but women seemed to love that.

My mother, Julie, or "Jules", as Del called her, was kind of wonderful and kind of awful. She was intellectually very clever, and talking about schoolwork or stuff in the news was always fun. She studied physics at Cambridge University. In her second year, she fell in love with a local 'lad' David, a buff footballer working as a barman. He was everything she should've avoided. She left university after falling pregnant with me and never looked back. When they tell that story, Del is proud, but I can't help but see a twinge of regret in my mum's eyes.

They always tried to outdo each other in fights and did not attempt to hide it from me. She would bring up his past failures, and he would always say he never even fancied her that much. In arguments, I've heard her scream at him that she 'only kept 'the baby' to stop him from fucking other women. His usual reply was that 'it didn't help much.'

I never thought that she had much control in her life. She went along with whatever Del wanted to do and eventually gave into him on everything, even when she clearly had reservations. She was far superior to Del intellectually but came out in the weaker position whenever they argued. All the times I needed her to stick up for me, she let me down. I wanted to go away on trips, science camps and solo camping to escape the family. I'd price them up, explain how I'd pay for them by working at the house or getting a part-time job, but Del thought they were pointless, and I should be with the family over Christmas, Easters and summers.

I don't even know why he wanted me around as we barely spoke to each other since the day I could first talk. Throughout the Covid lockdown, I've spent about twenty hours a day in my bedroom, and neither of them bother coming up to check on me.

I always wonder why mum stayed with my dad. The most rational reason I came up with is out of fear of being alone. Her Mum, my grandmother, was alone most of her adult life after her husband died a few years after Mum was born. They never had any money, and the loneliness turned to bitterness as she got older, according to what I've picked up from conversations I've heard. Mum says grandma was depressed and died young because of it. I guess this must have impacted mum a fair bit.

Del's parents lived a few hours away. He was the youngest of four brothers. We never saw any of his side of the family. They used to fight a lot growing up, and I think it spilt over one day to the point where Del never went home again.

Recently I realised that I was an island, a solo entity, a castaway but still reliant on the mainland that is the family. I needed to find a way out. I started working on the plan during the school year. The idea was risky and perhaps quite revolutionary. I was just starting to get everything together at the start of the summer, but an unforeseen entity entered my life and seemed hell-bent on distracting me. When she arrived, everything changed.

3

This year the worlds destiny had been defined by the pandemic, but I wouldn't let it define mine. Since we went into lockdown, I revelled in solitude, glad not to be in school. For me, school was a mixture of idiot children and idiot adults scrapping for attention or some semblance of power.

I lived and went to a school outside the big city, where no one got shot or stabbed, but school still wasn't short of its scraps, and the usual testosterone-fuelled nonsense. Some of the boys had an older cousin or a friend they 'grew up with' who lived in the city. They'd inevitably have been arrested or did drugs, but above all, they were always dangerous. The rest of us were warned and should be very scared. Before fights happened, a threat to call their cousin to come to school at the end of the day was chucked out into the row. This technique was used to exert some power for the kids that had massive egos and nothing to back them up. Because of these scare tactics, properly bad fights were rare.

I had a few friends; I wasn't a total loner even though it might have looked like I was. I guess the most obvious was Neil, whose mum was friends with my mum, so we got pushed together from primary school. I didn't think it was necessary for us to be mates just because our mums were but he seemed to love it. We were inexplicably put in the same form every year since joining secondary school. Every new year I got into class, Neil would see me and immediately sit next to me, putting us in each other's pocket for the rest of the year. I did find him funny on occasion, but he just didn't have the intelligence or imagination to fathom the kinds of plans I was making, so I didn't share too much with him in the last few months. Neil would invite me to things that I might not have been invited to, which was, useful I guess. I never considered him best friend material, though. He was just too grubby for the image I was trying to cultivate. At least once a week, he would completely clear a room just with his flatulence. I have no idea what he ate to create these bionic farts; it must have been an allergy to something. I always knew one was of his atomic air biscuits was on the launch pad because he would make sure all the windows in the classroom were closed before people sat down and settled. Everyone needs their own niche, I suppose, but I'm not sure where that's going to get him in the future.

I excelled in all the sciences. This might have brought some negative attention my way from bullies, but luckily, there was a kid in my form who was extremely fat and extremely ginger. The double whammy. On top of this, his parents committed the ultimate offence of giving him a first name that was actually a second name and could also be used for a girl, Monroe. Giving a child a name like that was child abuse, in my opinion. Monroe took a lot of flack. Sticking up for him was kind of pointless because it meant sticking my own neck out. He wasn't very interesting to hang out with, so why would I be friends with him?

The thing is, I never felt singled out or bullied by anyone because everyone was delivered brutal abuse on a daily basis. The fewer friends, the less abuse you got, which was also a good motivation for me to keep my social interactions low. I didn't like pointing out other peoples weaknesses, especially not the obvious ones. Nothing was off the cards. Boys were openly racist, homophobic and would even rinse someone if their parents had worse jobs than what they thought was good. Mo's mum works on the till at Waitrose, and he gets constant shit about it. Personally, I didn't get it.

The best way to make friends outside of those in your class was by being in a team, but I hated sports. First of all, I really hated running in general. Sting sung 'a gentleman will walk and never run' in his track Englishman In New York. I liked that and always tried to keep to that rule. Also, I grew up seeing how much of my dad's life revolved around sport, so it turned me off further. I didn't see myself missing out on any camaraderie either. The boys in the football teams were friends, but it never evolved into something that looked like team pride.

My school had the worst football and rugby teams of any school in the area, but the team members got let out of class to go to games. I saw it as just another way for the less intelligent pupils to skive.

To add insult to injury, my school was all boys. No girls.

Ashcave Boys Tech was an all-boys school. I assume this made it different from a mixed school in many ways. For example, I'm not sure there would be a drawing of an erect, veiny, ejaculating penis on every desk, chair, bench, locker and toilet door if girls attended the school. I'll admit to having even drawn a few myself. It was an unspoken challenge to see who could sketch a stonking chode the quickest after someone had cleaned one off during their Saturday detention. The most perfect canvas to express yourself on was brand new school equipment that had only just been delivered. On school trips, the coaches windows looked like a modern art collage as soon as condensation had the balls to rest. Cocks, dicks and willys were drawn in every style imaginable. Ashcave Boys Tech was a remarkably average school but I genuinely believe that this is where we excelled. If it became a competitive event akin to playing football against other schools, Ashcave Boys Tech would have claimed a world title in penis drawing for sure. It's the only sense of pride I had for the place.

There was a general atmosphere that no one, especially the teachers, cared about anything. The only emotion showed by them was absolute disdain for most of the students. It must have been a policy the school had for recruitment that stipulated all the applicants must hate the job of teaching, hate all children and most definitely hate themselves. These were the minds left in charge of moulding ours.

Even though I knew I could breeze through school if I wanted, I pretty much gave up just before we broke up for Christmas last year. The final straw broke after a run-in with Mr Branach. He was an angry Scot. He ticked an extra box in the child hatred section of the job application form. I got the feeling that he hated the English as well. Yet the subject he chose to teach was English in an English school. Mr Branach used to come up with his own creative kind of punishments and emphatically lose his temper on a daily basis. I felt he had no reason to lose his temper with me as I never gave him reason to. That's what I thought anyway. I was quiet, punctual and always did my homework. In the same week he had Neil work on the floor by his desk, 'Where the pigs live!', I did my homework as usual for an assignment set by the school. An essay titled "Where do you see yourself in 5 years?". The assignment was obviously designed to keep the students focused on their exams and university prospects, as that's what schools of that calibre were judged by when ranked. They weren't tasked with producing well balanced, informed and confident people. Schools were creating idiots who did well at learning misinformation and false history for tests. I had no intention of sticking to a plan set out by a bunch of adults who were deeply unhappy with their own lives. So I opened with something to that effect in the first paragraph of the essay. I explained my plan of escaping the present situation that I felt I was condemned to waste away in just like everyone else and what I really wanted was to travel to a future where philosophers and scientists were once again respected and in charge, like in ancient Greece. It turns out I needn't write beyond the first paragraph. Mr Branach started his shouting with what he considered a dressing down, attacking how I looked, how I carried myself and my lack of friends, then moved onto my parents, who I sensed he was strangely jealous of. None of which bothered me in the slightest. I remained emotionless throughout the bollocking. When he had stopped, I said, "It wouldn't happen again." and smiled. What I meant was that I would never do a piece of homework again if it were just going to end up like this. Wasting my time. I stuck to it and got plenty of detentions right up until we went into lockdown, which actually played right into my hands... Plenty of time to focus on my escape plans.

4

By the time we got round to March, my parents were nicely annoyed with me, mainly because of the detentions I racked up but also my 'general passive-aggressive behaviour'.

School went into lockdown because of Covid 19. I watched on as everyone panic bought toilet paper, including my parents, even though we definitely had enough to see us through several years. I stayed at home while mum went to the shops, raiding the supermarket shelves for hours for rice and pasta. I didn't fancy fighting a middle-aged woman over a packet of Uncle Bens ready-made risotto that would probably stay in the back of her cupboard for so long that her grandchildren would eventually find it in her post mortem house clear out.

I hadn't failed the year yet at that point and could still lie to my parents about school attendance and progression whenever they showed a glimmer of interest, which wasn't often. I attended the zoom classes, but I skipped doing any of the homework. Instead, I did other boys work for them and had them pay me via a Monzo card I set up.

It was announced that my year wouldn't have to sit the mock GCSE exams, and we would be put into next years sets where our grades from the year put us. Until Christmas, I mostly had A's and B's, but since I refused to do homework, my grades plummeted. The school let my parents know via a letter. Any excuse to berate me was leapt upon by Del, who I don't think even took his GCSE's. From that moment, I made sure to intercept all correspondence from the school.

Soon into lockdown, my parents planned events for when they were allowed to leave the house again. Del decided to book a holiday with my mum and some of his mates as soon as the lockdown ended. Mid June, they went away to the coast for a week and stayed in a big house all together with no kids. I was palmed off to Neils for the week.

The school was 90% closed, but Neil's mum made us go in because she had to work, even though she was still doing so from home. We didn't have any proper classes. We were the only ones there and had to work from an itinerary the same as everyone working from home. I didn't believe anything could be stupider than school usually was, but the way everything was organised during lockdown really showed how wrong I could be. I had my homework business working well over this time. Everything was typed out and sent via email, so no one had to show working or show their handwritten notes. I saved up plenty of money leading into the summer.

The end of term came soon enough, and I finally had some time to start putting the plan I had come up with during lockdown into action. I ignored my parents' letters from school instructing them on finding me a summer school to get my grades up to Year 11 levels for the next year. I wasn't going to be attending Year 11, so no need for all that.

In an attempt to work some kind of a holiday out for me, Mum suggested I go away with a friend and their family. The only friend I might have gone with was Neil. His family were going to North Wales for two weeks. That sounded like a long drive to go somewhere with terrible toilet facilities and worse weather than where I already was. 'No thanks' was the answer. I had a lot of work to do if I was going to be ready to escape before the return of school in six weeks.

My bedroom was the base of operations. I cleared away the posters of different nebulas taken by the Hubble telescope and replaced them with false blueprints I'd made as a decoy so that if mum came in snooping around, she'd see what I wanted her to see. The real blueprints were hidden in the gap underneath the last drawer of the chest of drawers. It had a compartment like a false bottom. I was sure Mum wouldn't look anyway. She was pretty uninterested in what was going on in my room. I kept it very tidy and took down sheets to wash on a bi weekly basis, so there was no need for her to come in.

At this stage, I had actually spent more time on the false blueprints than the real ones. I needed time and privacy to complete the proper ones. The decoy plan blueprints were easy to come up with because they were so ridiculous. I'd bought the garden shed from Del over lockdown with the money I earned doing other students homework. I figured out I could get extra metal from the local scrap yard or, at the very worst, steal car doors from the locals (I never worked out how I would do this but was motivated enough if worse came to worst). The false blueprints made it look like I was building a sauna in the shed. Del loved the idea and didn't even question it. Apparently, it makes perfect sense for a 15-year-old to want to build a sauna in a garden shed over the summer holidays. The sauna cover idea was genius, if I do say so myself. It would use many of the same parts as the invention I had actually planned to the untrained eye.

In my bedroom was a double bed against the wall, a large pine chest of drawers (with the false bottom) and on top of it was my toiletries. Last year I saw the film American Psycho which inspired me to rethink my whole morning routine, it took longer than it used to, but it was worth it. I smelt the best out of all my classmates, which wasn't a huge feat but something to be proud of nonetheless. Del would not be amused because my moisturiser and after shave was much more expensive than his. I emptied out cheaper brand bottles and filled them with my more expensive ones, so he didn't see my products and steal them or ask me money questions. Trying not to be seen spending the money you have is actually quite tricky. I can see the value in a top-class accountant when you're a drug smuggler. Hiding a few hundred pounds was hard enough, let alone millions from the government!

Next to my chest of drawers was a cupboard. Normal set up there, apart from the false back I was about to stick in it. The room that I'd get from putting in the false back would be a good place to stash bigger items.

My desk sat at the end of my bed. It was too small to work on my blueprints. I needed a big one that I could stand at, but it would've been hard to bring in the house without suspicion.

Before properly getting to work on the blueprints, I needed to make a list. Seeing as this lab or 'chamber' had never been made before, it would be a little trial and error. So first, the basics.

- Shed
- Metal lining (Preferably chrome)
- Airtight seal

This was a good place to get started before I ordered in some of the more complex hardware. I had the shed, and everything else on the list was readily available. But the new desk for my bedroom was something I wanted most. I went online. Found the perfect one. Delivery time was very important. Del was back on the road working, so he was out a bit, but he couldn't be at home if something got delivered because he opened packages that weren't even for him. It would be even better if mum wasn't home either, but there was no chance of that. It was while I was filling out the order I got called downstairs. It wasn't a shout for dinner because I had a big lunch, so I knew I'd be eating crisps for dinner.

Del was swigging a beer looking very happy with himself. Mum was sitting at the kitchen table with her diary out, writing something down. Del spoke slowly and arrogantly like people were just going to listen regardless of him making eye contact. "Great news Pad's" He hasn't called me by my name since I was born. It's always been Paddy or Pads, even though he knows how much I hate it. I leaned against the doorframe of the kitchen and waited for this inevitably terrible news.

"Barry Sedgley is coming to stay for a few weeks while he's on business." It looked like he was addressing his beer rather than me until he glanced over, waiting for my response as though I was supposed to know who he was talking about.

I didn't see why I had to be called down to hear this. "Great, who's Barry Sedgley?" I asked to keep him happy.

"Bazza! Sexy Sedgy!" This is how my dad spoke. Like I was supposed to be on his wavelength at all times. "My best mate from school. He left just after you were born when him, his wife and daughter immigrated to Australia. She was born a little while before you."

"That's brill, dad.' then I thought about the implications. 'Staying? What, here at the house?"

"Yeah, of course. It'll be fucking great to have him around. He's hilarious! No holds barred. Some of the dirty things he used to do..." He stopped his train of thought, seeing his audience wasn't interested in getting into storytime. "And Lucy his daughter. She's not been back since she was a baby, so you can show er'round. She's got no friends here, so she'll have to hang out with you."

I knew this was a masked dig so I peeled off the doorframe and walked out, back upstairs. I could hear my mum asking, "why did you have to say that?" I didn't hear his response.

I was anxious with the news of the imminent arrival of house guests! I made it up to my room and to the foot of my bed, where I sat for a while. New people in the house over the summer was going to be hugely inconvenient. This girl would be here during the days when I was going to have the house to myself. She was going to want to bother me when I should be working. She'd snoop around my things and slow me down, or, worse get me busted. But slowly, my thoughts changed course; What if she was gorgeous and I fell in love with her? What if I lost my virginity? She's pretty much an Australian girl even though her parents are English, and she's never met a British gent her own age. Foreign women love English men; that's a fact.

Having lots of sex all summer could get in the way of my escape plans. I'd been working on them all term, I thought. I wasn't going to let some stunning Australian model take my attention away from what really mattered...

5

The next day I woke up after a restless night. I got up at 7 am, the same time as I would if I had school on that day. Routine is very important if you have a task to complete.

After getting dressed, I headed down to the kitchen where my mum was making a cup of tea. She was fully made up in a skirt and blouse. Very unusual for her at this time in the morning.

"Good, you're up. Your dad will be back in a minute with Barry and his daughter."

This news hit me like a bus. Throughout the night, I thought that this idiot and his daughter were going to come and screw up my plans, whilst at the same time making up a small workout routine that I could insert into my morning schedule so I would look cut for her arrival. My feelings about the arrival of Barry and Lucy were torn because of some improbably sexual fantasies I had dreamt up and the actual disruption they would cause in a few weeks time. That was right up until I found out they were coming that bloody morning! The immediate arrival was an injection of stress like I'd never felt before.

I hadn't done any press-ups, so I had to get some in before they got to the house. I wanted that fresh pumped look. I'd never had it before, but I'd seen a lot about it on social media. Apparently, your muscles look their best a few minutes after a workout. The one issue with this was that I'd be sweaty again and have to go through my morning routine again. I panicked that they would have arrived just as I was getting out the shower and Del would make me meet her while only wearing a towel. He would do that. Even with a fresh pump that would still be embarrassing. I rushed through the work out of twenty press ups, thirty sit ups and doing bicep curls with my ruck sack full of books. The following shower had to be a few degrees colder than usual to cool me down. I started my skin care routine again but this time I skipped the exfoliating. No need to do that twice in one morning. I'd end up with grazed skin then more spots will turn up.

I finished my hair for the second time, unstyled looking but very deliberate. It was a challenging look to maintain as Del's lad mates always wanted to scruff up my hair when they saw me. That messed up all the work I put into making it look unstyled. The wax I used holds strands of hair together just tight enough to curl them a bit. If something like a dirty unwelcome paw ruffles the waxed hair, they separate, leaving them out of place, looking like fluff. Fluffy hair isn't a look I can deal with. Then there was the noise of a car pulled up into our drive. I looked down, and it was Del's Audi.

Everyone got out of the car and walked to the house. I couldn't see her face. She was wearing a woolly hat, in July. First of all, I ached at the thought of her being a skater, and that woolly hat being a permanent feature. There isn't a section of society I hated more than skaters, especially the most recent incarnation. They're all listening to hip-hop and talk like they grew up in Compton, LA. The cultural appropriation seems a little on edge for me. They think they are insanely cool because they're definitely not racist. They all think they're so subversive because they travel around on a plank of wood stinking of BO and whatever makes hair dread.

It occurred to me quickly that the woolly hat could just be because she was from Australia and probably thought this barmy 22-degree morning was cold. She's also wearing a thick tracksuit. All pink but not like a child. It actually looked quite cool. It was hard to tell what sort of physique she had.

They were in the house. I'd go down when I got called to keep it casual. I expected Del to shout up and get me to help with the cases, but I could see he was bringing them in from the car and taking them inside himself. I waited for a couple of minutes, but he never called me down. It was like he'd forgotten I was even in the house. I waited for about 10 minutes. The longer I left it before going down the tenser I grew. The temperature outside was heating up quickly, which only made me sweat more. I caved and went down before I needed a third shower.

They were in the kitchen. Del was hyper. I could hear it in his voice. He was swearing a lot which was a giveaway that he was either nervous or excited. I walked in, making sure I didn't look at her straight away. I make eye contact with my mum, who stood at the back by the kettle.

"Paddy, this is Baz." Finally, I met the almighty best mate from school, Barry. He was everything I'd hoped for. He wore jeans, a golf shirt and flip flops. The tattoo on his arm was of a woman's name. Aimee - The way you spell it if your parents are posh but not so posh that they give you an old fashioned name like Meradith or something. He must have been punching above his weight with Aimee, hence the permanent reminder on his arm that he did something in his life worth remembering.

"Hiya, kid" Baz didn't go for the hand I held out but instead pulled me in for an extremely uncomfortable embrace, including a rub on my head. I was smiling on the outside and fuming intensely on the inside. I turned my head to see and make first eye contact with Lucy.

"This is Lucy, Barry's daughter", Del beams.

"Yep, I figured that out." That was the positive/normal response I went with. I shook her hand and gave her a nod of the head. It felt a bit like when we had a drug enforcement police officer visited school, and I shook his hand. I felt a touch of pity come from one of us through the handshake, and I'm not sure which direction.

She didn't say a word. Whilst still shaking my hand, she used the other to cover up a yawn. She had a face like a model but not the Instagram kind, the high fashion kind, slightly weird looking but also kind of beautiful. Her face was thin but with exactly symmetrical lips. They were full and thick, like two pink slugs laying on top of each other. She looked tired and like she didn't want to be there. A feeling I sympathised with.

Mum finally entered the conversation to give me the task I knew was coming. "Can you take the luggage up to the spare room?" I dutifully obeyed. "Barry, we're going to make the dining room into a bedroom for you. At the moment, you can sleep in the spare, and Lucy can have Patricks for the night."

Halfway up the stairs, mum shouted for me to bring down the "dirty sheets". Dirty! They went on two days ago! How dirty could they have gotten? I wasn't doing anything dirty in there. As I stripped the bed, I began thinking that I should be glad that Lucy probably thought I was gross. The most important thing during the summer was to stick to the plan of escape. Truthfully though, I knew that I didn't want anyone thinking I was gross. I didn't need that legacy left behind. Of all the possible things people could say about me for the final word to be "yeah, but he was kind of gross" was literally the exact opposite of what I was going for.

I got rid of the 'dirty sheets' and replaced them with a 'clean' set. As I finished up, Lucy stood in the doorway, looking past me and out the window. I didn't have time to get out my plans from the false bottom under the chest of draws I had left open after getting the sheets out. I hoped she wouldn't be asleep for too long so I could get on with things in the afternoon.

"Here you go, all yours." I held my arm out, presenting the bed. This wasn't how I imagined it would be finally getting a girl in my bed.

"Thanks, Pad" I didn't correct her. I'd have to the next time otherwise this would be a permanent name. She slinked by me and just laid on the bed, face down. I did the gentlemanly thing and pulled the blackout blind down. She let out a grown. I assumed it was a thank you.

My hopes of Lucy taking a quick nap were dashed. She passed out for 14 hours straight. I had to sleep in the dining room on an inflatable mattress meant for Barry. The dining room was in the corner of the house next to the living room and the kitchen on the other side. The position of the room meant I could hear what was going on throughout the bottom floor of the house and what was happening directly above me. Lucy was finally awake. I could hear her clomping around and then coming down the stairs. She came and woke me up, even though I wasn't actually asleep.

"Pad..." She whispered.

I stayed still. It was too hot that night to sleep in PJ's, so I was sleeping in just my boxers and didn't have a fresh pump on. I didn't think I needed to. Just calling my name wasn't enough for her. She actually came in and trod on the corner of the inflatable mattress, moving the whole thing so much I almost rolled to another side.

I groaned for a second, then said, "It's Patrick."

"What?" Her nasal Australian accent was so thick, even with just one word.

"My name. It's not Pad. It's Patrick."

"Your dad called you Pad earlier."

"No, he called me Pads, short for Paddy, a name some people call people with the name Patrick. But I prefer just Patrick. He knows that."

"Awe. Sorry mate" She called me 'mate' within 10 seconds of the first conversation. I knew this would grow tiresome.

"Don't worry about it. You have a good sleep?"

"Yes. Yes, I did. Out like a light. I'm absolutely starving now, though. I didn't want to raid the fridge without asking and everyone's asleep."

I knew I was going to have to get out of bed. I had been clenching all my muscles underneath the duvet since she walked in, in the hope of getting some sort of a pump on.

"I'll show you where everything is" She turned and walked out. I leapt out of bed, and threw on a plain white t-shirt. That with my blue boxers looked something like a proper outfit.

She was standing next to the fridge, looking eager. She was thin. Quite boney, actually. "You can look inside, you know."

She smiled and said, "You can't just open a strangers fridge. You need someone to open it for you."

I liked that she was polite. These unwritten rules are what separates the good people in this world from every other moron. I opened the door, and she went headfirst into the light. She was still wearing the tracksuit bottoms but was now in a baggy t-shirt, no woolly hat. Her hair was quite long but not quite down by her elbows. The colour was strawberry blond, darker at the roots, lighter at the tips. She had these active thick eyebrows leaning over her cobalt blue eyes.

"I don't know anything you have in here. What's good?" She asked while her head was still deep inside the fridge.

"What would you eat back home?" I replied.

"Oh, I'd kill for some avo on sourdough toast." She looked for a positive reply, but I had to let her down for the first of many times.

"Sorry, but we haven't progressed as far as having avocado's regularly in our fridge, and the closest you'll get so sourdough toast is the sliced bread that's in the freezer." I stopped and remembered, "There's some Ol' Del Paso guacamole that's been in there since last summer, I think." She was unresponsive apart from some short "hmmm's."

"There's ham, and that's where the salad stuff is." I pointed at a salad crisper that looked bizarrely ancient, like my grandparents passed it down as a family heirloom. "Also, we have copious amounts of mature cheddar." She pulled her head out of the fridge.

"That spells out a toastie to me." Her smile beamed. Her teeth were completely straight apart from two of the bottom left ones that crossed over each other, disrupting the perfection.

"We actually have a pretty amazing Breville toasted sandwich maker in the cupboard. I'll grab it." When I brought in the Breville, she sat at the kitchen table and waited for me to make it. Not even flinching to offer a helping hand. All part of being the guest on the first night, I assumed. We didn't talk at all while I made it. I put it in front of her and went to bed, leaving her alone with the toasty. I went and laid back down on the inflatable. I couldn't get back to sleep for a good while. I should have shown her how to work the TV and the Wi-Fi password, but it was too late. I couldn't go back in randomly; she'd have known that I was in the room thinking about her.

6

The Cryogenic Freezing Chamber, which I would name The CryoShed, was the answer to all my problems. Scientists have been researching and experimenting with this technology for years. The most recent evidence was that freezing a person or animal of any sort would end with the subject turning into a soggy mess once thawed. Something to do with the cells in the body crystallising. This didn't put me off because, as I read on the Cryonics Institute's website, future technology will be far beyond ours, so that this wouldn't be a problem. Everyone saw the trick where you put a fly into the freezer and bring it back to life from the warmth of your hand. My logic was that clearly it's not impossible to reanimate. I trusted that scientists in the future would be able to wake me up safely. I've also read somewhere that there's going to be a way to download someone's consciousness onto a hard drive pretty soon, so in 100 years, if needs be, they'll just do that and put my consciousness into a robot body. I wouldn't mind being a cyborg; I imagine cyborgs have boundless energy. Not sleeping would be useful when it comes to getting work done. That's probably the way humans will evolve. No sleep to spend more time working and more time watching TV if things carry on the way they are. On a side thought, I'm banking on an awakening, a global acceptance that reality TV is awful. My thoughts are that this change might come after the ice caps melt, permanently flooding most of the beach resorts. I had noticed that most of the reality shows either take place by the sea or have people on them that come from places near the coast. Drown them, and that should purge the world of reality TV, the silver lining of global warming as thousands - maybe millions will die.

The one thing that concerned me was that I'd be tampered with by random idiots who don't know what they're dealing with. To stop that from happening, I drafted up a letter that would be left in my bedroom, on the front of the chamber and timed to email everyone once I went into freeze mode.

Do Not Disturb D1 Patrick Waters

I, Patrick Waters, have entered into a cryogenic sleep that mustn't be disturbed for 100 years. This letter will serve as instructions and as a goodbye to my family. Mum, I'm sorry to leave you. I think you tried to be a good mother, but you could have done better in all honesty. Dad is an intolerable idiot. Just staying with him and making me live with him is a serious laps of judgement. Saying that, I do love you, and maybe you'll live long enough for us to meet again. I'll be the same age, but you'll be 143. Dad, I told you I don't like being called Paddy every time you did it, but you continued. I'm growing into a man, so I feel like one of us had to go and, as it's your house, it should be me. When I bought the shed, this was the plan. You're not getting your sauna, I'm afraid.
I'm taking anything important with me. Everything else can be binned.

This venture needs to be kept within the family. Secrecy is paramount. The repercussions of people finding out could be harmful to the country and the world. My cryogenic freezing will attract attention from the media and cause a stir at school.
Only one month before the 100-year freeze is anyone allowed to reveal what's happened.

Yours Sincerely
Patrick.

The wording needed work, for sure, but so far, so

good. I put this on hold while I carried on with the technical aspects of The CryoShed.

I was going to need liquid nitrogen. And lots of it to keep frozen for 100 years. The chamber itself would have to be small so I could get the best use of the liquid nitrogen. It should repel the heat and keep the cold in.

All in all, the idea was there. It just needed finessing. The design of the chamber I'd be laying down in within the shed should be simple. It would look like one from the movies but less glass. Cold escapes from glass very quickly. I would need a window so people could see in, and I could see out when I woke up. It would only be lockable / unlockable from the inside, but I'd put a handle on this outside as well because my muscles might be in atrophy if the thaw took longer to work out. Regardless of the what-ifs, something told me a handle on the outside of the chamber was a good idea. I thought dripping the liquid nitrogen onto the metal shell would mean staying at a constant temperature below zero. So I needed something to drip it and a machine to pump it out in tiny amounts. I was sure that Google would have all the information I needed. In the meantime I had to clear out the shed of all the crap.

I couldn't work on The CryoShed for a couple of days as the guests got settled in, so I was getting anxious at my lack of progress. On the third night of sleeping on the inflatable mattress that was supposed to be designated to Barry, I was determined to do some work on the shed. The fact that I no access to my own room was adding heavily to the anxiousness. So getting Barry out from sleeping in the spare room and into the dining room was my second priority of the day.

Upon waking up and doing my sit-ups, I went into the kitchen. It looked like I was alone in the house until I spotted Lucy with her head in the fridge again. She must have heard my bare feet walk towards her on the laminate flooring. She lunged out, holding up two avocados.

"YES!" is all she said. Putting one back in the fridge and turning to crack into the other one.

"How are you doing today?" I asked.

"Good, thanks, mate. Feeling like I'm waking up a bit now," She was very awake for 7:30 am.

"Cool." I was consciously keeping thing chilled between us. I didn't want a friendship this summer. The escape plan was the priority.

"What you doing today?" She asked while struggling to slice open the thick black skin of the avocado with one of our blunt kitchen knives.

"Nothing exciting. Clearing out the shed." I shrugged.

"Aw. Can't you do your chores another day? I want you to take me exploring England! I've never been here!"

"My dad said you were born here." I pointed out.

"Oh yeah. Except for then." She was now concentrating on smashing her avocado.

"I thought people visiting from Australia had to stay in isolation for two weeks?"

"Yeah, supposed to, but we're not going to. Look, Barry's already gone out."

I didn't like the rules being broken, people were dying, and all that people needed to do was obey a few simple rules, and things would be fine.

"It's actually not a chore. I'm doing it for me. I bought the shed from my dad, and now I'm getting rid of his stuff." I wasn't sure if she had heard me or just stopped listening because I didn't get a response for a few seconds. She looked up at me like she was going to say something, but there was just a weird silence. I was quite stiff and stood there wondering if the conversation would start again. It didn't, so I turned and walked out.

7

The shed hadn't been opened since the end of last summer, and I couldn't really remember what was inside. It was heavily cluttered, but most of it could be chucked. Del had already agreed that everything inside the shed was mine. It raised the cost even though he knew it was all tat. I knew it was important to buy everything in one go otherwise Del would make me rehouse all his junk.

Just so I didn't throw away anything useful, I unloaded it all onto the grass in the garden and made an inventory list.

Shed Contents:

- 3 Buckets of various sizes.
- Wire fencing.
- Broken petrol lawnmower.
- Push powered lawnmower.
- A barrel of blue rope.
- Swingball minus the ball and rackets.
- Badminton kit minus one net pole.
- Seventeen tennis balls (loose).
- One bowls kit (only one ball in the kit).
- A plastic gnome.
- A clay duck.
- 30 roof tiles.
- A bag of pointing sand.
- A neon Budweiser sign with no cord or plug.
- Three fold-out chairs.
- A shovel.
- A garden fork.
- A pick.
- A Irish hurling bat.
- A car radio.
- A carrier bag of nuts and bolts (mostly rusted).
- A wicker basket with two troll dolls and six loose

marbles.

- Three sheet metal cigarette advertising boards from the early1960's.
- 5000 cobwebs.
- One giant spider.

Lucy watched from the kitchen for almost all of the time and stood next to me while I made the inventory list. She didn't say a word even after I said hello and asked her if she knew that 'avocados were actually berries?'

Everything was in an organised state laid out on the grass. Lucy was sitting on one of the fold-out chairs with her beanie hat back on. I felt intensely uncomfortable having her eyes on me. My arse was clenched, and my stomach was aching as I'd held it in for hours. She did not attempt to put me at ease. Whenever I turned and caught a glimpse of her, she was looking right at me. I started to think, well, hope, that she might fancy me, but the look she gave me wasn't one of lust.

Now the list was made, I decided what to keep. The rest was getting binned. The adverts and the neon sign would go up on eBay as they looked quite cool and in decent condition. Del probably nicked them from somewhere, I thought.

As I loosened up the bags and went to indiscriminately chuck stuff in, starting with the Irish hurling bat, Lucy piped up.

"Aren't you keeping that?"

"Nope."

"What are you doing with all of it?"

"Chucking it. None of this is worth anything?"

"It's all worth something. Nothing is worthless."

"Actually, yes, it is. Nothing is worthless, and this is nothing." I was holding up the bat and stuck it in the bag.

"I reckon I could sell all that."

"No, because then we'd need to keep it somewhere."

"Why don't we just keep it in the shed till it's sold?"

"I need the shed empty. That's why I've cleared it out."

She didn't say anything. She was out of her chair and looked in the shed. After being inside for a few seconds, she started to push the walls from the inside. "Not very sturdy," she shouted from the inside of the lurching shed.

I was in a slight panic that she would push through the wall and create more work but I let her test it out because part of me was curious to see how sturdy it was. Nothing happened, which was a good sign.

Lucy stepped out. "Can't see many people being able to fit in once it's a sauna." She had clearly taken a look at the fake blueprints. "What are you really doing with it? You don't seem like the sauna type."

I stepped into the shed. "I've worked it out, and with the raised platform on the inside here and here", I pointed on the left and right sides of the inside of the shed and spread my arms in a smooth motion, "you'll be able to get two people laying flat and two sitting up, or six people sitting up."

"Hmmm. Yes, I saw the drawings," She said, beginning to lose interest.

"The blueprints."

She shrugged. "Yeah. It just doesn't feel big enough."

"Well, it is. And I need to throw everything away. I've not got time to be messing around with selling stuff I'll only make a couple of pounds on."

Lucy shrugged her shoulders and went inside the house. I binned everything and dragged the bags up to the wheely bins stuffing them in, hoping that the bin men would still take them like this.

8

Everyone's eating schedule had been off since the arrival of Barry and Lucy. We eventually all ate together on day four. I brought up the topic of room switching so I could get back in my bedroom, but it fell on deft ears. The fact that I was totally displaced and had a girl sleeping in my room with all my stuff in wasn't an issue to anyone else but me. The dining room had literally no privacy. My parents kept all the extra crockery, cooking books and stuff in there because there isn't room in the kitchen cabinets, so Mum was in and out of there all the time. With Lucy walking around the house at random points, I had no time to masturbate in comfort during the night. I was down to about one a day, and that was from the toilet before I had a shower. It never used to be part of the bathroom routine, and now it was the most important part. I used to fit a wank in while I was still in bed in the morning before getting up, one at night before I slept and one in the daytime whenever I needed it. The comfort aspect was now out the window. I had to sit on the closed toilet seat with a bare arse on cold plastic.

Now I was paranoid it would look strange to spend a large amount of time in the bathroom, eventually rousing suspicion. I figured that it looked like I was either wanking or taking three or four shits a day. Neither was something I wanted Lucy or my mum to think. I was tenser because of this drop off in my 'sexual' activity. Lucy was quite comfortable in the house now and mainly wore very small shorts and a hoody. The shorts were baggy but came up so high that the round underneath part of her backside was on show whenever she walked by. I could see the crease that linked the bum to the legs... This only added to the tension further.

Del was back on the road working and came in every evening boasting about how well things were going. 'Selling more than before Covid.' Apparently, people wanted to insure themselves more now everything was at risk of going down the toilet if they get hit by the pandemic.

At breakfast, Del suggested I take Lucy out into London for the day, right in front of her. Never once in all of my life did either of my parents ask if something was alright with me privately before publicly 'asking' me to do something that I most certainly didn't want to do. I'm not sure if this was just them being inconsiderate of my feelings or if they knew by asking in advance it would give me more time to make an excuse; it was probably both. Fortunately, I did have to pick up some parts for The CryoShed from London. But how could I do this with Lucy watching my every move? I wasn't going to go all the way into Central London without a plan of action. I promised to take her out to London in the next day or two. Today I had to go to the hardware store to pick some roofing up because the one on the shed wasn't going to hold for the next few months, let alone a hundred years.

The hardware shop was about half an hours walk. Everything was about half an hours walk from our street. It's a residential area built in the '60s when everyone either had cars or was going to. Some houses from the '60s were still around, but most of them had been knocked down and replaced with two or three, smaller, more modern houses. I really liked the old houses. They were bigger and looked much cooler. They had massive windows at the front, and you could see all the way through the house if the curtains were left open. The newer ones all looked the same. Redbrick, some brown wood, four windows and a front door. No one ever tried to customise them at all. The only difference was what car was outside.

I walked up to the front door of the hardware shop and stuck my mask on before walking in. In truth, I liked wearing the mask. It meant that I didn't have to appear too cheerful and could carry on in a monotone without insulting anyone. No one knew that I wasn't smiling.

"Hi Ranjeet, Do you have the roofing?"

"I think it came in yesterday. Let me check." He ducked out into the back office. The shop wasn't very big and as far as I knew he was the only person who worked there so he must have known if an order came in straight off the top of his head, but he had to make a bit of a song and dance first.

"Yes, it's here. It's quite big."

"How big?" I called over the desk.

"How big? You should come and see it." He held his hand out to the door frame and waved me behind the counter.

I walked around the desk, and he showed me into the office outback. When I got back there, what I saw wasn't exactly an office like I had imagined. It turned out it was just a big cupboard full of folders and other accounting type looking things. On the floor was the roll of roofing I'd ordered. It was indeed big. Larger than I had thought as I'd only ordered a few meters. Getting it home was going to be a drag, literally.

"Thanks, Ranjeet. I guess I'll drag it home."

"Drag it home?' He shook his head. 'You won't drag it home. You'll break it apart." The truth is I didn't actually care about this roofing or if it broke apart. It was going to be covered up with sheet metal as a second protective layer, anyway. Even still, this was going to be difficult to get home. I propped it up on one shoulder like I'd seen scaffolders do with large polls. As I turned right out of the shop, I tripped at the door step, dropped the asphalt on the floor, and watched it roll on the pavement. I stepped out to grab it, and standing to my right was Lucy. She had followed me. I had no idea, and this scared me a little. I stopped, and she watched as the roofing dropped off the curb and settle in the gutter.

"It's new roofing for the shed," I said after it stopped moving.

"Yeah, I guessed that. Need some help getting it back?" Lucy asked.

"Yes, please. That would be great, actually." I said, extremely relieved to have some help.

"Cool."

We both picked up the roll and carried it up on a shoulder each.

"So you followed me?" I asked.

"Yeah, well, you ran off. And I'm getting bored in that house now" That was the longest sentence I'd heard her put together since we met.

"Sorry. I just remembered I had to get to the shop to pick this up. I didn't want Ranjeet to sell it."

"Don't worry. I understand. You don't know me, don't want to hang out with me."

"No, it's not that. I mean, yeah, I don't know you."

"Seriously. Don't worry about it."

We walked for about ten more minutes swapping shoulders a couple of times. The roll of asphalt was getting seriously heavy now. I was sweating so much it kept slipping from my grip. I felt like a weakling because Lucy didn't seem to be struggling at all, but it was getting too much for me. "Can we stop for a bit?" I finally said, panting slightly.

We were right by some grass. In one motion, she dropped the roll and fell to the grass, letting out a long gasp! "Oh my god. I was struggling there." She started to laugh, seeing that I was sweating through my shirt.

"Me too," I laughed exhaustedly. We sat, and for the first time, I felt some comfort around her. "So, did you want to do something tomorrow then?"

"Yeah, if it's not a pain. I don't want to make you feel like you're my babysitter."

"Cool. Where did you want to go?"

"How far is Camden? I've always wanted to go there."

"Why? Camden's a dump, and it's about an hour away on the train."

"I love Amy Winehouse, and she lived there. It would be cool to just check it out. I've read there's markets and stuff?"

I knew this was really going to eat into the day. The specialist for the liquid nitrogen I wanted to visit was in Kings Cross. That wasn't too far so I could go there as well. "Ok. Camden it is."

"Have you got any mates you want to bring?" She was already picking up on the fact I didn't like anyone just by mentioning the concept of friends. If she knew the pool of people I had to choose friends, she wouldn't be surprised.

"My mates are on holiday at the moment."

"Just the two of us then." The smile she gave me was warm and accepting, like she didn't care that I was a loner and that she liked me anyway. I struggled to think how I would keep her at arm's length when I was already beginning to fancy her. I started to seriously worry that falling in love wouldn't be the problem this summer and the real issue was me falling into the friend zone faster than anyone in history.

We made it home eventually, after a few more breaks. There was no one else in. We rolled the asphalt down to the shed and went back up into the house. Lucy went upstairs, and I went looking for food. Cold sausages leftover from breakfast. They did the trick. After eating, I went upstairs to get some privacy. Watching Lucy walk for the last hour had stirred something up. I opened the bathroom door, and Lucy was standing there naked, drying herself off with a towel. I stood for about a second, and she covered herself up. I slammed the door shut.

"Sorry! Sorry!" I called.

She didn't reply. She opened the door a crack and was fully wrapped in the towel. She was smirking. I guess enjoying the fact that I was uncomfortable and apologetic. "Don't worry about it." She said with her face poking out through the gap in the door. "You get a good look?"

"Barely. Sorry, the door wasn't locked" I was doing my best to keep my cool.

"You want to see me again?" What the hell was going through her mind? Who cared, because I definitely wanted to see more of her. I was stiff all over as soon as she asked me.

"Erm, yeah," I replied.

She opened the door up a little bit more and unwrapped the towel, keeping it in one hand. I didn't want to act like a total pervert, so I looked at her face with my eyes darting all over the rest of her. She was thin. You could make out a few of her ribs. She had small boobs but they weren't completely flat. They were nice, I thought to myself. She kept her pubic hair in a tidy triangle, not very long. I was taking mental photographs until she turned around laughing. The towel was back on after only a second or two. I was sweating again. The door shut. "Knock next time!" She said from behind the door.

Was this a sign I wasn't in the friend zone? What zone did girls flaunt their bodies at you? I walked quickly straight to my parent's ensuite bathroom and was out of there before Lucy was even done drying herself off. I went back out to the garden to unwrap the roofing, and I looked up at the house. Lucy was starring down at me again from an upstairs window. She smiled, then laughed and walked away.

That night we had dinner. All of us. I was extremely tired. I just wanted to eat and head to bed to watch YouTube documentaries. Lucy was sat next to me, and I was opposite Barry. I felt anxious around them both. Before, I blamed his quietness on the jet lag, but they'd been here almost a week at this point. He only really looked at what he was eating or at Lucy even though she wasn't saying very much. My mum asked Barry's about his wife back in Australia. Barry didn't say much; it seemed to me like something was up there. I assumed that maybe they were having marriage trouble, and that's why he's over here with Lucy, taking a break. Del wasn't as talkative tonight either. The vibe around the table felt tired.

After dinner, Barry borrowed one of the cars to take a drive with Lucy. They were going to where he used to live when Lucy was born. It was somewhere about an hour away. I pointed out it would probably be dark by the time they got there. He ignored me, and they went anyway. Del offered to drive, but I think Barry was getting bored of reminiscing and wanted to escape. Lucy seeing where she came from was a good excuse.

The inflatable mattress was impossible to sit on comfortable, so I was lying uncomfortably in my temporary accommodation and mum and dad were talking in the next room. Mum sounded totally pissed off. I could hear Del do his usual of calming her down and then ignoring what she was saying, then cutting her off mid-sentence. Mum didn't like Lucy walking around the house, not wearing much. She busted Del looking at her before dinner. That explained the mood, then. What was he supposed to do, though? Tell Barry his daughter was skipping around the place, making his wife jealous? That'd be a fun conversation. I also took issue with this, as looking at Lucy was an enjoyable part of the day I didn't want taken away. Besides, I felt like Lucy and I had made the foundations for a possible connection and I didn't want my mum causing any kind of aggravation. If Lucy felt like she wasn't free to be herself, she might not feel free to climb into bed with me randomly in the middle of the night. So far, that's the only way I could see us having sex. The showing of her naked body was a way of getting control of me or just to mess with my head, I was sure of that. Approaching her about it or trying to kiss her was still miles away in my mind. If I went up to her room and tried to make a move, it would be a creepy teenage boy overstepping boundaries. I would get branded as a sex pest, but for her to do it would be fine. More than fine, I wished it would happen! It was definitely a long shot.

I went for a wee before going to sleep. Del and mum were in bed. Barry and Lucy were still out. When I came out of the toilet the car pulled into the drive. Barry and Lucy were laughing in the car. I thought it was good they went to see something to do with Lucy's life. The engine turned off and they kissed in the car before getting out. It looked strange. It was on the lips and milliseconds longer than what a kiss between a father and daughter should be. I thought to myself this was strange but when I got to bed I thought how much of a disgusting perv I was for thinking that its weird. I don't know how father and daughters show affection. I'm looking at her from a position where jealousy could creep in. Was I jealous of her dad giving her a peck on the lips? The guilt of thinking that sat heavily over me. I felt pretty sick because of that guilt and also because I genuinely felt jealous, I needed to get a grip of myself! They came in the house and tried to keep quiet. I listened by the door. Didn't hear anything though. I went back to bed and imagined more fantasy ways in which Lucy would want to have sex with me.

Thoughts of ways to seem cooler and sexier to Lucy was now at the forefront of my mind. The CryoShed had already dropped slightly out of focus.

9

The next day I woke up determined to get back on track with my planned escape. I decided that going to Camden was off the cards. Getting everything I needed and ensuring the shed's revamp didn't raise suspicion was my sole focus.

It was a Friday, so I had to get to the metal yard before lunch because Phil, the guy who had been letting me into the yard to rifle through the junk metal, got drunk on his Friday lunch breaks and would just want to talk to me for hours about his troubles. He got me once before. I was flattered, to begin with because he asked me about my life, but it soon became apparent that he only asked me about mine so I would ask about his.

Phil waved me in, looking up from The Sun newspaper for a few seconds. Next to him, he had two empty Rustler microwavable burger packets. I'm guessing that was his breakfast. I went past all the wrecked cars down to a pile of metal scraps that were there waiting to be sorted through.

One pile I was going through had no system to it but was full of gems. I needed some thick cast iron to make the chamber that I would use to create the hibernation pod. To begin with, what would be perfect would be an old industrial stove with a metal door and window still intact. Last time I was there, I saw one and pretty much based my blueprints on it. I shifted old radiators and railings around to find this stove in the same place as I discovered it. I started to regret not coming up here a few days ago. Just as I was giving up, I found it. We were back on track.

I removed all the scrap from around the stove, and as I uncovered more, it grew in size. I thought this was a stove from the way it looked underneath all the crap, but it turned into a different beast altogether. There was a pressure gauge on the side and valves. I had struck gold. I had no idea what it was originally used for, but with some modifications, I could fix it to the shed and fit in it no problem.

Getting it back to the house undetected was going to be hard. I couldn't move this on my own and I thought that might have been the reason why it was still in the scrap yard. I'd struck gold with no way of mining it! I piled metal back up over it and went to speak with Phil, who was just about to leave for his lunchtime piss up. He didn't really want to hear about the unidentifiable chamber that I found. I had a feeling he knew about it, and from our brief conversation, I gathered it wasn't going anywhere anytime soon.

On the way home, I got a cab to take me to pick up some insulation and a lot of thick tinfoil. I had to get the shed walls prepped for holding in freezing temperatures.

Back home, Lucy was in the garden sunbathing. Our back garden was in an L shape, with a slope from the back of the house down. A patio at the top and the shed down the bottom. I stood at the top of the garden, looking at Lucy. Mum wouldn't be happy with seeing Lucy dressed like this. She wasn't in a swimming costume, just a bra and knickers. I wasn't really sure what the difference was between wearing a bikini and wearing underwear, but I knew there definitely was a difference. It just felt, naughtier. The straps of her blueish bra moved down below her shoulders, and she laid on a bathroom towel as she read one of my books. She heard me shuffle around and turned her head, not quite looking at me.

"No Camden today?" Her Australian accent made it hard for me to tell if she was annoyed with me or not for standing her up.

"I had to get some things sorted this morning, and time ran over. Sorry."

She just stayed still. It wasn't just the accent that made it hard to tell her feelings; it was also impossible to tell from her mannerisms. She just looked the same all the time, no matter what she did.

I pulled the insulation over to the shed. Lucy didn't

flinch or look up from the book as I dragged the 15-meter roll across the garden. As I walked back into the house to grab the tin foil, I saw my mum come in through the front door. Straight away, she was on to me and waved me over to her.

"You have to entertain Lucy, Patrick. I know you don't want to be tasked with anything, but you have to do your part around here." I nodded subserviently. I followed her to the kitchen, and saw mum looking at Lucy from the window. "Just get her out the house for a while, please."

"Okay. Tomorrow we'll go into London." Mum was just looking at Lucy, not saying anything. "Can I have some money, though?" I didn't want to spend my own money if I didn't have to.

"Yes, take £30 from my purse so you can get some lunch."

"Thanks, mum" £30 for lunch wasn't enough for the both of us. I figured Lucy would have her own money.

In the shed, I lined the wall with foil using the heavy-duty stapler. Even though the foil was the thicker stuff, I doubled up on it. By the end of the afternoon, I had stapled insulation and foil to the whole inside of the shed. The sun was starting to dip, and once it came in low enough to get into the shed, it would be impossible to work in there because it was so unbelievably bright. It was like a hall of mirrors but with no gaps. Light reflected off of every surface. It wasn't hot though, which was reassuring. The tinfoil was creased everywhere, so I found it uneasy staying in there. Just as I was packing the stapler away, Lucy came to the shed wearing more clothes.

"This doesn't look like any sauna I've ever seen."

"It still has a long way to go."

"Looks cool, though."

"Thanks."

"You've got some food ready up there."

"Cool, thanks. So you want to head into London tomorrow then?" I was packing up and not looking at her for a reaction, but I could tell she wasn't happy with me now.

"You're not going to run off again tomorrow morning?"

"No, I'll wake you up and have a plan, I promise."

"Ok." She walked off.

I had thought I was babysitting her, to begin with, but just a look and by the tone of her walk, she managed to flip it around to make me feel like she was doing me a favour.

I went up to the kitchen where my mum had made a massive chicken Caesar salad for everyone to just take what they wanted out of the bowl. I grabbed a plate and fished out as much of the chicken as possible without it being too noticeable. This wasn't going to fill me up after the day I had. I looked in the fridge eyeing up some bacon to fry to add to the meal when mum came in. She saw me and walked over to me.

"Can I talk to you for a second?" I figured I was in trouble for not taking Lucy out earlier.

"Sorry I wasn't here this morning. I had to do some stuff."

"No, that's fine. Let's talk in the other room." So this was a private talk.

We were in what was now my temporary bedroom. The dining room with the blow-up bed. I sat on the mattress and bounced around for a second, getting comfortable. Mum sat on a chair.

"What's up?" I asked when I finally stopped bobbing about.

"Nothing really."

I knew immediately this meant something was massively bothering her. So I was just going to let her say it in her own time.

"What do you think about Lucy?" She asked with a tightness in her jaw.

So this was it. Lucy. That's what was bothering her. I thought my mum was above being jealous of a teenage girl.

"How do you mean?" I wanted to keep my opinions vague at the moment. Telling mum that I was pretty much infatuated with Lucy wouldn't go down well.

"She seems strange to me. I can't put my finger on it. Barry lets her behave how she wants. She's very quiet around me, but I've seen her talk to you. What has she been saying?" Mum held her look onto me, and I honestly didn't know what to say. Lucy was strange, but ALL girls have ALWAYS been strange with me, so I met fire with fire and acted strangely back. Was Lucy abnormally strange? She flashed me her naked body the other day. No other girl has ever done that. I decided not to mention that particular interaction, however.

"She's quiet, but I think it might just be jet lag." That's the best I could do under these pressures.

"See what she says about home. Ask her about her mum."

"Okay, sure. Why?" This was especially random behaviour from mum. She was usually unfazed by people. Lucy had clearly irked her.

"I can't. Me and her mother met once. She's a very jealous woman and assumed because I knew Barry from his early days that we must have had a thing because all women must fall in love with Barry." Mum rolled her eyes.

I was left stunned by this. Was Barry some kind of a ladies man back in the day? It was hard to see past his greying hair and beard. He was quite thin but not athletic, from what I can see. He barely engaged in group conversations most of the time but seemed fine when he did speak, even though he never said anything that struck me as intelligent.

"Okay," I said with no real intention of following through.

"Are you out with her tomorrow? I need the house back to myself for a while tomorrow."

"Yeah. Taking her to Camden. Will be out all day probably."

"Good." She grabbed my hand and squeezed it, and left. She had her faults but I did love her. I thought I should probably be kinder to her in the note I leave when I freeze myself. As mum walked out, she bumped into Barry coming in with Del. They had been drinking after work, and there were big hugs being chucked around. I stayed out of their way. I knew mum wasn't in the mood for this, but neither was I. I poked my head out after a while, and it was just Del, Barry and Lucy with a bottle of wine. Mum must have been upstairs steadily getting more annoyed.

I had to report back to mum with something in the next few days. She would stew on this. So the next day was about two things. Trying to forge a relationship that would somehow lead to sex with Lucy and get some information about her that my mum could chew on for a bit.

10

We got a lift to the station from mum. Lucy made her thoughts clear as soon as the car doors were closed and mum pulled away. "Urgh. Your mum, mate." Then a looked at me. I looked back, waiting for her to finish her sentence, but that was it. It was enough. I thought the way this outing was starting out it would be an extremely awkward day, but everything was fine as soon as we got on the train.

The conversation on the train was about where we were heading and what Lucy wanted to see when we got there. Amy Winehouse was spoken about again. I didn't know anything about her apart from that she died. Lucy was obsessed. So the mission for the day was to go see Amy's old house and the statue of her. A selfie at each was important.

I had been to Camden twice before when I tagged along with people from school. The first time Neil invited me and made me bring a bag so he could buy a bong and sneak it round to his at a later date. The second time, a load of people randomly decided to go after lunch on a Friday and ditch the afternoon classes. I only had a free period, and PE left, so was fine with bunking off.

I can't say Camden had a huge effect on me the same way as it did for literally every other teenager. Even on the tube, I could tell who was going to get off at Camden Town. Grungers had things hanging from their clothes like vines that break away from trees, key chains, festival bracelets, piercings and laces dragging on the floor, the grunge uniform. Goths... no need to go into too much detail when describing a goth when two words is fine - all black. Blatant stoners wearing hoodies and beanies in August. They wore sunglasses all year round, which was finally passable now it was summer. And of course skaters, we kept our distance from them.

Mixing amongst all these cliches didn't agitate me as much as it usually did. That may have had something to do with people looking at Lucy and me, assuming we were together. Sad, I know, but it gave me an ego boost, even though it felt like I was light years away from having sex with her.

The journey there was much less busy than the other times I'd been. Everything was much quieter. I hadn't really noticed much of a difference in life while staying in Ashcave, but the post-Covid lockdown in London was different. Nicer now there weren't random strangers rubbing up against you on a packed tube.

We got to Camden Town at about 12:30. Lucy was eager, grabbing my hand and dragging me out of the tube station. It might have been a bit quieter, but it was a million miles away from being deserted. There were still plenty of tourists, teenagers and drug addicts wandering around.

Lucy was smiling like a kid opening up presents on Christmas. I'd only caught a glimpse of this smile a few days previous when she saw avocados in the fridge.

We walked down past the chain shops weaving around beggars, drunks and pierced punks handing out flyers. I was scared of catching hepatitis from even touching one of the flyers, let alone Covid, but Lucy grabbed all of them and stuck them in her bag. If she suggested she, or worse, we get a piercing, that's the point I would have gone home without her.

This short walk took about half an hour just because of all the people. Tourists were stopped looking at their smartphones, comparing Google maps with the paper maps they had bought. From memory, I eventually got us to the first market area. Lucy stopped at the very first stall. She started trying on band branded t-shirts. Amy Winehouse, Nirvana, Korn, and, I guess ironically, Spice Girls. She bought an Amy Winehouse t-shirt and put it straight on, instead of the one she was already wearing, carelessly taking her shirt off in the middle of the market with people looking at her in her bra.

The next stall had the worlds largest display of terrible jewellery. They did their best with the covic precautions and made sure Lucy squirted antibac on her hands, but that wouldn't stop those crap rings from turning your skin green if you wear it for too long. Lucy bought two rings and a necklace after I agreed what she had picked out looked great. She wasn't into haggling, straight in there with cash, which she seemed to have plenty of. The Australian Dollar to Pound exchange rate must have been good to her, or she saved up before coming over, or she was just a spoiled child, but I didn't pick up that from how she was or how she dressed. Maybe she had a job. The fact there were all these questions over her made me feel even more obsessed. All men looked at her. Guys my own age were obvious, but older men still had a long stare when they thought they weren't being seen, and it made me jealous. Not a feeling I'd ever felt before. It made me feel weak and out of control. I ground my teeth to fight the feelings giving myself a headache. Pretending to be confident today would be an Oscar-worthy performance, especially as I didn't know where to go next.

We walked further down the high street, going into almost every shop. Talking on the way, I asked her why her mum didn't come with her here.

"Ah, well, I don't speak to my mum that much," She said casually like it wasn't a big deal.

"Why not?" I pushed. She paused for a second, looking at some huge leather boots with spikes on.

"I mean, I speak to her but not that much. Not since arriving here."

"You've not called her? Does your dad talk to her much?"

"Yeah, of course. It's just difficult with the time difference."

I nodded and didn't think about it anymore. What more information did my mum want? "Do you want to get some food now? We can eat from the market?"

"Let's go to a pub!" She grabbed my hand and pulled me out of the shop.

We walked over to The Oxford Arms, which was a couple of doors down. I was positive if we looked for even a few seconds longer, we'd find somewhere that didn't smell like chip grease, stale beer and old man farts. I wasn't sure if we were allowed in a pub on our own, so I had a familiar feeling of imminent ejection anxiety.

As soon as we walked up to the door, we had to wait to be seated. A waitress looked at us suspiciously and showed us to the only available table at the back, by the window and explained it was table service only. She left, and Lucy and I sat in silence. I was sure we'd be asked to leave any second.

A Spanish looking barman with a chessboard patterned sleeve tattoo came over and talked to Lucy. I zoned out and watched the two of them. If I were to describe the exchange would say this was textbook flirting. Exact procedure taken from flirting advice I read on the internet. Lucy was playing with her hair, and the guy was leaning in. Eventually, she pointed at the beer tap and asked for two pints. I thought she would get away with it until I saw him look over at a barmaid, who mouthed "IIII...DEE". The tattooed barman then asked to see Lucy's ID. I started to get up, ready to leave, but Lucy got a card out of her purse and showed him. He looked at it for a few seconds, and they began flirting again. He gave the card back and went to get the drinks. This was amazing.

"You've got ID?" I asked her.

"Yeah, fake obviously." Of course, she had a fake ID. Girls always have a fake ID. The few girls I knew or had contact with wouldn't hang out with us because they were already going out to clubs with their fake ID's. Or that's what I had figured out. The last house party I went to was full up of older guys who knew the girls that used to come to our school discos. They all met from being out. All my attempts at going out had ended up sitting in the 24hr McDonalds, wishing I was at home instead of avoiding eye contact with the harder boys in town. To me, the nearest McDonalds was the only one in Surrey that had bouncers on the door all weekend. As long as you had some fries or nuggets, you could sit in there all night, so it was a meeting point for all the kids who tried to get served in one of the 20 pubs or bars and got denied.

We were halfway through our pints and had ordered some food. Lucy paid for the food and the beer. She talked about the differences of pubs in Sydney and that the beers never came in pints but were always ice cold. She thought these beers were warm. I didn't even like the beer but drank it anyway. I felt the effect of the alcohol laughing at her describe how small you could get beers in Australia, not something I wouldn't usually find amusing. She drank hers in the time I drank half. Our food was on its way, but she wanted another one, so she ordered another couple of pints on her way to the toilet.

While she was in the loo, the guys on the table next to us turned round to me. They were a few pints deep by the looks of the glasses piling up on their table. They were two LADS. Like younger versions of my dad. Short back and sides, with the only difference between them being which direction their quiffs pointed.

"She your bird?" Left pointing quiff asked while right pointed quiff leaned in eagerly.

"No, not really." I wasn't scared of these guys, but I knew I hated them, which made me feel vulnerable. I was just hoping that Lucy wouldn't find their muscles and manicured beards charming.

"She's lovely" Right-sided quiff pointed out. I took a casual swig of beer and just raised my eyebrows in agreement.

"Yeah. What she doing with you?" Both quiffs laughed.

"You even old enough to be in here?" Left quiff thought he was hilarious even though I wasn't actually old enough. I didn't say anything. Lucy came back over with two more pints. She sat down, looking at me then the two quiffs.

"Hi. We were just asking if you two are from around here?" Left quiff had completely changed his accent and persona in an instant. I'd seen this many times before when my dad spoke to different people. Switching from a cheeky down and out lad to acting completely differently, speaking the queens English when speaking to anyone of high status.

"I'm from Sydney. First time around here." Lucy replied, but I sensed she was just being polite.

"I'm from Surrey." I said.

"Sydney. You're a long way from home, aren't you, sweetheart?" Right quiff's attempt at being charming was grossing me out, and I was getting more concerned about Lucy's resistance to this type of bollocks.

"Yeah, we can show you around, hun." Left quiff started to move his chair over towards us as he offered his tourism assistance.

"Please stay over there. I just want to talk with him, thanks." Lucy just dealt a blow to these two I did not see coming. Left quiff wasn't put out, though.

"You sure? We will make you feel welcome." He flashed a grin.

"I'd rather you just fucked off and left us alone." Lucy spoke loud enough for the barman to notice.

The two of them looked to see if anyone was paying attention. "Alright, sweetheart. Calm down." Left quiff moved his seat back.

"Silly bitch" Right quiff said at full volume. Lucy wasn't satisfied with just telling them to fuck off and gave him the finger just as our food came up. I needed to go to the toilet as the beer had gone right through me, but I was too scared to go in fear of one or both of these guys following me and giving me a pasting. Lucy kept talking, but I was just listening to the two lads decide where to go next and find more girls. Once they left, I ran to the toilet. I got back, and Lucy was talking to a random couple. She was finding out about where the Amy Winehouse memorial was and where else we could go that's cool.

It was surprisingly sombre at the Amy Winehouse statue. As we got there a couple of girls around our age were there with some flowers. If we timed it differently, we could quite as easily have gotten there when a dog was relieving himself on it. Nonetheless, I felt a bit sad this talented singer died so young. Lucy actually shed a tear. I used this moment to try and make the first contact. I went to hold her hand. She held onto me for a good three minutes, but I knew I'd have to let go before the clamminess turned to sweaty, moist hands. We stayed for about 5 minutes overall.

We walked to another pub where I stood outside, and Lucy got the drinks. When she came back, I got a feeling she was starting to like me. She came out with a takeaway pint in each hand and a smile. We kept eye contact the whole time until she gave me one of the pints.

"Thanks for hanging with me today." She smiled.

I felt incredibly relaxed. "No problem." I smiled back.

"What's next on our adventures?"

"Not sure. I've got to build the project in the shed. I've been planning it for ages."

"Are you going to tell me what you're really doing in the shed? You just don't seem the sauna type."

I gave a rye laugh "What's the sauna type exactly?" She swept back her hair. This was it. We were flirting. I was sure of it! She laughed with me. I couldn't believe it. I was flirting with a beautiful girl while drinking a pint outside a bar in London. If you had asked me two weeks ago if this was likely to happen, I'd have laughed but not like how I was laughing now. This laughing felt great. We drank the rest of the beer and chatted more. I avoided talking about the work I was undertaking in the shed, instead diverting the conversation to Scandinavian customs of being naked in the sauna, and that's something to look forward to when it was built.

I had her in the palm of my hand. I was sure that this is what dates were like, and it felt like she liked me. She was annoyed I didn't spend time with her, so she must have liked me even before today. Why wouldn't she like me? I wasn't bad looking, I knew a lot of interesting facts about science, I had my own money, I didn't wimp out with those guys earlier, and she clearly thought I was funny. That's what girls want, right? All this was going through my mind as she spoke about the summer in Australia being so hot they don't need saunas.

She finished the drink and leaned over to me. I went for it. I don't know why because, as it transpired, this was out of the blue for her. She dodged my kiss, and my mouth landed on her shoulder. She stepped back.

"Pads, I have a boyfriend. Sorry." The sorry was definitely pity based.

"Patrick, please." That was my response to being rejected. I look back and feel proud of that. I was drunk by then, so the next day, I could blame it on that, but I stayed true to myself by correcting her about my name.

Of course she had a boyfriend. Strange how it only just came up. I felt the need to get details, but she was looking concerned after my correction. I downed the rest of the pint in one.

"Cool. No worries, mate." I said in a mock Australian accent. She wasn't impressed. I carried on regardless. "What's he like, love?"

She exhaled exhaustively and put her gangly arm around me, and we walked back towards the high street.

"He's older, and it's a bit complicated" She didn't say much else and neither did I.

I was carrying her bags but gave them to her as we entered the station. I had to go over to Waterloo to buy the liquid nitrogen from a guy I met online, but I was feeling tired. I mentioned I had to go somewhere, but Lucy quashed it and dragged me with her. She had her arm around me on the train. I wasn't enjoying this close contact. I was pissed off. I knew that after today I was definitely friend-zoned.

On the way home, she spoke about how great the beach was in Sydney and about how fresh the fruit is. Her obsession with avocados was less adorable after half an hour of drunk waffling about them.

I text mum to pick us up from the station. She knew something was up as I was annoyed and quiet, and Lucy had her eyes closed for the whole way back. When we got home, I took three packets of hula hoops from the cupboard and went to my room. I was sitting on the inflatable mattress eating crisps when Mum came in to get a report. I wasn't in the mood.

"Hi darling... What did Lucy say while you were out today?"

I turned over and pushed my laptop to the side

so I could still see what I was watching. "She said she doesn't speak to her mum much and that she has a boyfriend."

My mum was perceptive. She left me alone after that.

I needed to find a way out of the friend zone. Lucy was going to be at the house for another couple of weeks. She was my only chance of having sex before waking up in the future. I had just recently decided that it was crucial that I didn't start my new life as a 115-year-old virgin. Just think of the headlines!

I stayed awake late that night imagining Lucy's older boyfriend surfing with dolphins until I pictured his surfboard getting chomped on by a Great White. It was about 1 am when I thought about stalking her on Facebook, but I couldn't find her. There were a few Lucy Sedgley's but none that looked like this Lucy. There was another one in Sydney, though, but I couldn't see any of her profile as it was private. She must have a profile in a different name. I didn't know this boyfriends name which meant I couldn't send him a virus, unfortunately. I fell asleep in a foul mood.

11

I woke up in the same mood I'd fallen asleep in. For once, it wasn't something to do with my parents or school. It was Lucy's friendship. I felt trapped in a place that had no escape like I had been airdropped into a maze where the exit was guarded by a beautiful monster who was too busy with something else to even bother with letting me out.

I stayed in bed rather than getting straight up as usual and started googling 'How to get out the friend zone'. The advice I found only infuriated me further.

www.onlinepsychologist.com gave a breakdown:

- "Be Less Interested" -

I'm happy to admit I didn't know anything about women, but I knew that openly liking someone was a good way of getting them to not like you. I don't know why. I'd kill for her to like me, and if she did, then I wouldn't freak out. Why would someone be uncomfortable with someone liking them? Still, I wasn't acting interested. I barely spoke to her. But I reasoned it would be best if I just completely ignored her.

- "Make Yourself Scarce" -

Okay, great advice. She's currently living in the same house as me.

- "Create Some Competition" -

This was a section about making her jealous. 'Start meeting other women and flaunt the new friendship in front of her...' This just wasn't going to happen. I had completely separated from all of my friends to concentrate on The CryoShed. Even the few friends I had didn't mix with girls. Lucy crash-landed into my life, and I knew that wasn't going to happen again with a new girl! It had crossed my mind that spending time with my mum might work, but I soon realised how epically desperate this course of action would be and not great for my mental health to resort to that.

- "Get them to invest" -

This was interesting. The article wrote, "Ask your friend to do things for you. Contrary to popular belief, people like you more when THEY do favours for you, rather than when you do the favour for them. This is called the Ben Franklin Effect (Jecker & Landry, 1969). The more they invest in the relationship, the more you will mean to them."

I had plenty of things that needed doing. I should find a way of getting Lucy to work with me on The CryoShed without telling her exactly what it was. I imagined how that would play out. We'd be working late one night, and I'd reach for a tool the same time she did. Our fingers would brush past each other. I would hold her hand and pull her in. We'd kiss for a few minutes and have sex in the shed. Perfect.

- "Be Rewarding" -

I became less cynical after reading this section and had some hope that I could salvage myself from the friend zone. "Don't forget to be grateful and reward your friend when they behave as you desire. After they are good to you, remember to be good to them back. Being attentive and affectionate, only when they do what you like, encourages them to continue those behaviours".

Now tackling this systematically with a plan was the way to do it. I couldn't make myself scarce or make another girl appear from thin air, but maybe I could twist her psychologically to get out of the friend zone and into a friends with benefits situation.

I had started to make notes on what tasks I can give Lucy to get her to invest in our relationship when Del came in. I was almost certain he couldn't read, but I closed my laptop so he couldn't see my notes anyway. He's lucky I had mellowed into a better mood since I woke up. It was Sunday, so I wasn't sure why he was in my room rather than playing football or watching it.

"Pads, we're going to do something today."

Del never wanted to spend time with me. Something was going on. Both mum and dad were acting strange with me this week, and it started to make me suspicious of something bigger going on.

"Aren't you playing football?"

"Seasons over."

"Why aren't you watching football with Barry?"

"There's no football or cricket on. Barry and Lucy have gone out for the day."

I felt stuck for the second time that day, and I hadn't even gotten out of bed yet. "What's mum doing?" I was desperately trying to find a way not to spend a day with him.

"She's got stuff to do today. It's just me and you with nothing to do."

A wave of rage crashed over me for a second. I had plenty to do, actually, I thought. He just assumed I was doing nothing. Not even a question of asking if I was available. Just his usual assumption that his weird son was gagging to kill the boredom of his existence with a generous offer to "do something" with his dear ol'dad.

"What did you want to do? I've got stuff I've already committed to."

"Shut up, Pads. Get dressed, and we'll go out." I would suffer because of some guilt Del felt because Barry was a better dad.

"Where are we going?" I asked.

"Let's grab breakfast in town and come up with a plan. I'm up for doing anything."

The plan was to go to a greasy spoon and for me to wait while Del read the whole paper. Followed by me making suggestions to go to the library, the cinema or shopping for parts for the shed "revamp", all to get rejected. We'd go bowling instead. Every time Del suggested anything, it had to take place where competitive sports and booze were under one roof.

At breakfast, the brief conversation focused on Lucy, much like when mum spoke to me.

"So you and Lucy are getting on okay?" Del inquired.

"Yeah. Fine." I answered, not wanting a slither of

feeling to escape.

"It's good that you're spending time with her. It's good that you're spending time with any girl I suppose." I wasn't sure if this was a jab at me possibly being gay or just pathetic. Either way, he said it with a smile, so he wasn't intentionally being a prick, at least.

"Do you fancy her?" A chill went down my spine. I looked at him. He was sipping tea and scanning the back page of the paper as he spoke. "She's lovely looking. I'm sure you're all over that" He looked up at me and winked.

The words "all over that" literally put me off my food. My dad, who's nearly in his 50's was talking about a 15-year-old girl like she was a stripper. But that isn't what angered me. It was the thought that he noticed that she was gorgeous and that he might be thinking of making a move and getting in my way. I wouldn't put it past him. He'd cheated on my mum in the past.

When we pulled up to the bowling alley, it was closed. The government were wise enough to understand that perhaps a lovely place for the virus to thrive would be the holes that get penetrated by the dirty fingernails and sweaty fingers of grubby blokes and their even grubbier children.

Instead, we just went to the pub, and Del threw darts pretty much on his own because I gave up after a couple of rounds. He was less annoying, probably because he gave up trying to talk to me, seeing as I hadn't responded to anything he'd said since breakfast. He spent a lot of time texting on his phone, and whenever I was within eyesight, he quickly pushed his phone into his pocket. He was pleased with himself for some reason, and it couldn't have been because he thrashed me at darts because we both knew that was going to happen.

We left after about an hour, and he had four pints. He was pretty drunk when we left and drove us home. I sat in the back seat, not risking it up front.

As we pulled into our road, I saw Barry and Lucy had also gotten home. They were in the hallway as we walked in. Dad gave Lucy a hug that lingered a few too many seconds for my liking, and I could see Barry wasn't impressed with it either. He actually put a hand on Del's back to signal the end of it. Del told them how he beat me at darts, and I retreated to my room. I didn't say hello to either Lucy or Barry. I had to "Make Myself Scarce" after all.

The day was like how summers were before I set out my plan to transport myself into the future, and this was what the next few years would be like if I didn't do it.

I needed a more disciplined approach to my work. I wanted to get every thought of Lucy out of my mind. She didn't like me like me. She had someone else. I wasn't in the friend zone; she just didn't like me.

Focusing on work would get me out of my current slump. I was doing great at the start of summer when all I wanted to do was build my cryogenic freezing chamber and wake up in 100 years away from the current state of my life. I would make sure to get back on that the next day, but for now, I went to my room and laid in bed, falling asleep to YouTube videos about serial killers.

It rained the next day - the Monday. The night before, I promised I'd start all over and get stuck into work. Instead, I stayed in my room watching YouTube and masturbated to porn stars that looked vaguely like Lucy. I hadn't showered or even picked up the blueprints to make the adjustments I'd thought of in-between YouTube and YouPorn tab switches.

It was, without doubt, a completely wasted day. I began to feel guilty for not doing anything by about 5 pm. I could hear my mum walking around the house, never crossing paths with Lucy as she came down to the kitchen for food. I knew the differences in their walk just by sound. They were equal in their avoidance. There was no way of me running into anyone today as I'd grabbed enough crisps and chocolate in one trip to sustain me for the day.

Before I fell asleep that evening, I googled symptoms of depression.

Search Results:

According to the National Institute of Mental Health, symptoms of depression may include the following:

- Fatigue and decreased energy.
- Feelings of guilt, worthlessness, and/or helplessness.
- Feelings of hopelessness and/or pessimism.

All it took was one weekend to make me certifiably depressed? I made a new promise to myself. Get up, exercise and don't google symptoms of psychological disorders anymore.

12

In a strange way, a day spent wallowing in my own filth and self pity was just what I needed to kickstart my get up and go. The next few days were great. I worked out a flawless routine, adding some new exercises to build strength. Astronauts had to be at their peak, both mentally and physically. I needed to be the same. I felt the effects instantly and started to think more positively. It helped that Lucy wasn't around as much. Barry hadn't worked the last few days and had been taking her out.

One evening I overheard Barry say to Del that he wasn't going back to Australia. I only assumed that his wife would relocate as well. But I didn't want to know; it wasn't my business.

The shed looked transformed after three days of solid work. Gone was the look of the wood panel exterior. I covered the wood with sheet metal I'd gotten from the yard. It wasn't matching, but it was all flat and nicely soldered/nailed together. I thought the patchwork look was quite cool. The main thing was that it was strong. The metal went down to the concrete, and I nailed it in so it couldn't be moved.

On the Wednesday I had a buyer for the old advertising panels that I had stuck up on eBay. I hadn't been paying attention to the bidding when I'd checked back into my account. I found that someone in America bought the lot for £7000 and had been messaging me about it for over a week. Obviously, I was shocked and fleetingly imagined what I could buy with all that money. But there was only one thing important enough to spend money on. The £7k was going to finish off The CryoShed!

I was thinking a whole lot more positively. On the Thursday I got a message from Neil. His family had got back from Wales a few days early because he accidentally flooded the AirBNB during an experiment with the bath and his Old English Sheepdog 'Stanley'. I didn't ask for more details; I just assumed the holiday was as boring as I predicted, so Neil got carried away amusing himself. He invited me to the park for cricket on the Friday. He said the teams were down a player, so they really needed me. He was back a day and had already gotten himself invited somewhere; no one had messaged me since we broke up for the summer holidays. Usually, I'd just see through this desperation for even teams and say no, but I was in a good mood, and the weather was nice. A day off around someone other than my mum would be a relief.

That day I was tidying away my work and hiding all the blueprints in their new place. I cut a flap in the back of the sofa in the living room, so all I needed to do was pull the sofa away from the wall and slide the papers inside, where no one looked. The sofa never got moved from that position, so the blueprints were safe.

Just as I moved the sofa back, Lucy came in and sat down. She didn't look great wearing her Beanie hat coupled with a jumper and baggy trousers. She had bags under her eyes and looked pretty ill. I turned to walk away, but she wanted to talk.

"How're you doing, mate?" She was looking at me when I turned around, and I felt that making myself scarce now would just be mean.

"I'm great, thanks. Everything is really good." Bit strong on the positivity, but I was feeling a lot better, so it was hardly a lie. "What about you?"

"Yeah. I'm getting a bit tired of being here. It's not like how I thought it would be."

"Do you want to come to the park with me and my friends tomorrow?" I asked her without thinking, immediately regretting it; What if she fancied some of the guys at the cricket and went off with them for the rest of the summer? What if she just decided to have sex with one of them in the woods while I'm fielding?

She sat up and eagerly responded, "Yeah? You sure?"

I couldn't change my mind now. Best case scenario is the guys think she's my girlfriend and stay away.

I started to feel very unsure of myself again. I felt her mood improve and mine plummet like we were on some kind of emotional seesaw. She invited me to watch a film, so I parked what I was doing and sat next to her. We spent about 20 minutes trying to find a film neither of us had seen, eventually settling on one we had both seen, Gattaca, one of my favourite films of all time.

Barry came in halfway through and sat with us. I felt a strange vibe from him every time I spent more than a few minutes with him. He slunk around on his own until he was around people, then his posture and attitude shifted to a confident persona that didn't match his appearance. The laddiness on show when Del was around never came out when Del wasn't there.

Friday was exceptionally sunny from early in the morning, and I gave my routine 100%. Barry was on his laptop in the kitchen most of the morning. I mentioned Lucy going to the park with my friends and me. He scoffed in a weird dismissive way. I was growing to dislike Barry on multiple levels.

Around 2 pm, Lucy and I left. The park was, like everywhere else, about a mile away. Lucy was wearing short shots and a vest. Even for her, this was skimpy, but I wasn't going to say anything. We picked up drinks that she bought with the use of her fake ID. It originally belonged to a girl she knew from school a couple of years above her. All Lucy had to do was buy a replacement one, and the older girl gave her this one. They did look very similar, unlike some of the fake IDs I had seen where the only similar attributes people share with their ID photo are that they both look human and have similar coloured hair. For girls, it didn't matter. Most places want girls in, so having an ID is enough fake or not.

When we got to the park, I had a vague idea where the people I knew would be. After walking towards the pavilion, I recognised some guys from the sixth form. I really didn't want to hang out with this lot. Especially not with Lucy. We got closer, and I realised they were all part of the cricket game I'd been invited to. The sickness I felt made my legs weak, which wasn't going to serve me well playing sports. I felt eyes on us as we walked over. I knew they were looking at Lucy, wondering who she was and what she was doing with me. They would have been wondering who any girl hanging with me was, I completely understood that, but a really hot girl dressed in barely anything would raise further questions.

The closer we got to everyone, the more I hated being there and wanted to leave. Turning back around and walking home would have made a statement. The mysterious persona I've been cultivating would go into hyperdrive. Annoyingly I had to keep up with Lucy, who was walking at quite a fast pace. I'm sure talking to other people apart from me and her dad was the main draw. She was smiling broadly and really stomping over towards the gang of boys.

The area of the park they dominated wasn't the actual cricket pitch. It was just off of the path towards the trees. This meant there was shade and places for people to hide while they smoked, avoiding the possibility of seeing someone they knew. There was space to play cricket but not a proper game, so I wasn't needed for numbers like what Neil said. He was just being nice.

"Are these your friends then?" Lucy asked. I had to start thinking about the meaning of the word friends because I deeply disliked most of the people in front of me. Neil wasn't even there. Without him there, I was sure that anyone else even knew I was coming. To be honest, I thought they might actually tell me to fuck off.

"Yep, this is them." I waved over at some boys from my year. Matt and James Castle were twins, and both were alright guys. I did both of their science homework for the last three weeks of term. They took the piss out of me but never in a mean way, so I knew I could at least talk to them. They weren't like typical twins. They were totally opposites. Matt dressed like he grew up in South Central LA in the early 2000s. He wore baggy jeans, a baby blue t-shirt and a Kangol flat cap. He loved 90's hip-hop and quoted lyrics from The Notorious B.I.G. all the time. I thought it was weirdly funny. His identical brother James was into fashion. He wore smart shirts and trousers with really nice shoes even now to the park. They lived with their dad in a small house; their mum had died years ago. That amount of testosterone living under one roof with no female influence and going to an all-boys school could've meant they end up a bit sexist or misogynistic, but if anything, it made them idolise women even more. They were really nice to Lucy without being creepy.

"What's happened to Neil?" I asked.

"He's coming. Think he's back from holiday today. He's been away since the start of summer. Said to me he's going mad with just his family." Matt was looking out for Neil as he said it.

"I know the feeling. I thought he was already back." I said. Then Lucy pulled out a bottle of wine from her bag, screwed the top off and took a big gulp. She wouldn't know that this looked incredible to all of us, and it stopped everyone from what they were doing. She was the sole focus of everyone there for a few seconds. She passed me the bottle, and I took a swig as well, knowing this looked insanely slick and totally out of character.

It turned out that one of the sixth form boys was supposed to bring the cricket stumps but then got grounded after crashing his car into his parents garden hedges. So about 20 guys were hanging out in the park in the sun, and Lucy and I were the only ones who brought alcohol.

I discovered this was what being popular felt like. Neil finally arrived and couldn't believe his eyes and was unashamedly by Lucy's side for the rest of the day. He wasn't the only one. Guys were queueing up to speak to Lucy, but she wasn't flustered by it, and no one was out of order. I was drunk and getting tired after a few hours. Lucy could handle the booze a lot better than me but when I walked off to pee in some bushes, she ran after me.

"Wait! Wait!"

"What? I'm going to pee in there." Pointing at the bushes about 15 meters away.

"Ok, I'll keep watch." She was drunker than I thought.

"No, it's fine."

"I don't want to be left with them." She said at full volume so they would have heard her.

"Fine. Just don't stand near me because it'll put me off."

She laughed, and I peed against a tree. Walking back over, she was hugging me, whispering and laughing. When we got back to the rest, we decided to leave and walk home. I felt like I had done wonders for my reputation that afternoon. Guys that I'd never spoken to before gave me hugs goodbye, probably just so they could do the same with Lucy, though.

My phone was going off as we walked away. Neil's Whatsapps was the only one I read. 'You've got to smash that man. Or at least finger blast! You can do it. She is in your house ffs! Let me know how she smells.'

On the walk home, we were both stumbling a bit. I was happy with the day, we had so many funny chats. Lucy and I were great together. Remembering what Barry said to Del about them staying, I thought that would leave an opening for me in the boyfriend gap as she wouldn't be able to go back to her boyfriend. I broached the subject.

"So your dad said you're staying in England now?" She didn't say anything. "What's happening with that?" She looked at me, stopped walking and dropped down to sit on the curb. Out of nowhere, she started crying. I felt guilty. I thought that she must be devastated about not seeing that guy ever again. I sat next to her and hugged her. Her face nuzzled onto my neck, and her tears dripped down on the skin of my neck and in between my shirt. I was so turned on by being this close to her and her wet skin touching mine. I didn't want to ruin it but thoughts of kissing her were forcing their way into my mind again. But before I put that thought into action, she took her head off my shoulder and cried into her hands.

"I've been lying to you", She blubbered. "I'm not Lucy. I'm not his daughter."

I was suddenly sober again. Wide awake. "What do you mean?" I asked.

"I'm not Barry's daughter. We left Australia together to be with each other." She looked at me to gauge my response.

I was intensely confused. What the hell was going on? What did she mean BE TOGETHER? Surely not in a relationship with Barry?

I vomited.

13

It took me a full 12 hours in bed, mostly tossing and turning, to get over the fact that Lucy wasn't Lucy and that she and Barry were effectively in hiding over here.

She opened up last night. These were the revelations: Her name was Rae, she wasn't Barry's daughter, she was his girlfriend. The thought of it made me very stressed and turned my stomach. As soon as I thought rationally, I thought that my mum was pretty much on the money, suspecting something was up with her. Should I have told her what I knew? I played out that scenario in my head: I tell mum. She flips out. Kicks Barry and Rae out of the house while simultaneously calling the police because Barry is a paedophile.

Unless Rae was older than 15. I hadn't gotten that information yet, and I wasn't sure how deep the lies went. Before I told mum and dad, I needed to get the facts straight.

For the first time in a while, I was alone in the house. A perfect time to start work on burying some electric cables in the garden leading from the house down to the shed. But I couldn't work. The sickness took over me, and so I just sat on my computer looking for missing person reports in Sydney. I didn't know what to think. They had been at ours for two weeks. There wasn't anything I could find apart from a private Facebook profile for Rae, second name Dextegen; I remember her revealing that the night before. Her profile didn't give any information, like her age, but I didn't find it that unusual. If you looked for me online, I'm pretty well hidden. Part of my plan was to almost vanish before I go into the freeze. This meant that clearing up my Facebook account happened a few months before. I know nothing is deleted permanently, the residue of all your online mistakes hangs onto the internet's sticky spiders web, maybe that's why they called it 'the web'? Luckily I wasn't the kind of person who had that much on Facebook in the first place.

I had been quite into Reddit for a while. I enjoyed reading the opinions that people from around the world had on every subject. It was on Reddit that I got the spark of genius to create The CryoShed. I was on a thread about India creating its own cryogenic device capable of sustaining 2 mill Kelvin, that's as cold as deep space. At the time of reading this I had already begun thinking of running away and starting a new life. So it was a well timed read.

Being only fifteen years old and running away from home meant that I would inevitably have to commit crimes or be involved in some kind of illegal activity or go into care and get chucked into some other equally shit school. If I ran away, mum would try to find me. She'd call the police and put on a search party. I don't think I'd get very far. I couldn't go to another country. The best hope for reaching another country would be to get a ferry to Northern Ireland and then go over the open border into Ireland. I could do it in a few days by buying bus tickets. If I chucked my passport and always used a false name then Ireland was my best hope for staying completely anonymous. What could I do when I got there? What kind of a person runs away to Ireland? I've never been but I imagine it's even worse than England. I've only had one proper interaction with anyone who's Irish. Shane at school had parents who were Irish and assumed I was because they heard me being called Paddy. They spoke very gently and quietly to me, completely invaded my personal space by getting in close and talking right next to my cheek. I couldn't stand it. Escaping to Ireland and running the risk of everyone talking so closely to my face wasn't worth it.

After my research into cryonics I didn't feel like running away was the best tactic and that freezing myself for 100 years for a better choice for me. During the initial research phase I of course watched some films on the subject but not all my info came from over stretched Hollywood narratives. I looked into what other people were doing in this area. The Cryonics Institute spoke about the 'the technology of life' but they still require you to die and then be frozen due to laws against encouraging suicide or euthanasia because you're technically dead if you're frozen solid but to my understandings people are technically dead during operations all the time, so I don't see the problem.

Rae's name was originally Swedish. That info came up randomly on Google, and it explained the looks. I started to wonder when her family moved over there. Maybe she was trying to get back to Sweden, so this was her route back. Sweden would be a bit of a shock after growing up in Sydney. It's in the dark for most of the year. It has the highest rate of suicide in Europe. It's not a place I would choose to run away to. It still trumps Ireland, though.

I had been hovering over friend requesting her for a few hours. What would be the big deal? She wouldn't see much about me as my photo is of the star V838 Monocerotis (V838 Mon) taken from the Hubble telescope in 2002. It's mostly interstellar dust from a past star explosion. It's extremely beautiful and is an exact depiction of how I see our place in the universe. Specs of dust. But my name is still there with a few photos I've been tagged in. I've deleted posts I made when I was 13 about Thor and Superman having too many superpowers in common. I was going through a Marvel vs DC phase that I'm over now.

As the morning went into the afternoon I began questioning my involvement in Rae's being here. If, for some reason, the police found out what was going on and came to the house to investigate, then would we be harbouring an illegal relationship? Every question I had eventually led to the question about what kind of relationship Rae and Barry had. I never want to jump to conclusions, but her words were "be together" when referring to why they were here.

My head was spinning all day. I had grown used to keeping secrets, but they were my own. Not telling anyone about my plan was made easier by writing letters explaining what I'm doing. Perfecting the post freeze narrative for my family to discover. This was a whole different ball game. I felt I needed to speak to someone. The problem was that I had cultivated a near-flawless state of isolation.

Everyone came home at once at about 6 pm. I wanted to look chilled out in case someone came into the room, so I started playing a documentary on Netflix about aliens building the pyramids. Only my mum came in to see what was going on. Apparently, I didn't look great - I thought of saying that I was hung over for only the second time in my life but just asked for a toasty and a cup of tea for dinner. I'd had enough crisps and Coca Cola for the day.

14

While I had been in bed, the wheels had been put in motion for a girls day out with Lucy (Rae!!) and Mum. I only found out when I was grabbing breakfast. Mum was making me a sandwich for lunch and casually telling me she was going to show Lucy around town in Ashcave. Show her what I didn't fully understand. At that time of the year, the shopping centre was mostly taken over by teenage boys desperately trying to make the girls laugh by dropping eggs off the higher levels and inevitably getting kicked out by security. I suppose it's more interesting than the rest of the year when it was a mix of single mums, pensioners and the mentally ill.

Something about Ashcave that is interesting is that it's a hub for the mentally ill. At the end of the 1800's it was decided by the powers that be that they should build six large mental hospitals or asylums as they were called back then, all within 15 miles of each other, all surrounding Ashcave. This became known as the Ashcave Hospital Cluster. Over the century, what was considered crazy changed, and there were fewer hospitals because the land they were built on became more valuable. Now I'm not saying that the opinion around mental health changed because hospitals were built on expensive plots of land, but it did help developers when there was less need for so many large hospitals. Could the word conspiracy be used? Maybe.

The area surrounding Ashcave was now mostly new build houses and flats. There was still a couple of hospitals in use. There was one hidden away in some woods that only a few people knew about. We found it with instructions from someone's older brother.

It was bizarre and scary to see. It hadn't been bought and converted yet and was just an abandoned hospital with a dilapidated mansion next to it. When poking around, we found some scary rooms and files on patients that had been left there, like the whole place was abandoned in a rush. We even saw a chair with leather straps attached to it in one of the basement rooms. It was pretty spooky.

Rae came down when mum was in the kitchen, ready to go. She was being very sheepish with me. I wondered if she was feeling trapped by the situation. She had cried for a bit with me after I threw up. What type of hold did Barry have over her? Was she going to open up with my mum like she did with me? That would have been the right thing to do.

It was just starting to rain when they left. I didn't get the opportunity to get Rae alone to ask questions. They came back soon after with Barry, who needed picking up from the station. They dropped him off and went back out to see Ashcave in the rain. So it was just me and Barry in the house.

Everything about him revealed him to be a stupid man who had dark intentions and no way of controlling himself. I didn't feel in danger, but I wanted to bring him down to a level of helplessness that Rae must have been feeling. I couldn't do all that in that one morning. Also, I figured Rae might end up being annoyed at me for rocking the boat before she had the chance to figure things out for herself. Barry tried to be friendly with me when he came in.

"Just us boys then? The girls out shopping, I bet." Barry spoke with a smile he knew was misjudged instantly. "What are you up to today?"

- I'm going to be in a police station making a statement about you, you dirty old fuck - I thought to myself. Even though I knew it wasn't true.

"Not much today. Got a few bits to do."

"With the shed? It looks incredible" He looked out the window at the shed, which didn't even look like a shed anymore. It was grey and metallic.

"Yeah, I'll work on the shed a bit today."

"I'm around if you need any help. I'm pretty good with DIY."

"This is a bit beyond your average DIY. It's got to be safe." I could feel myself being deliberately arse-hole'ish to him. I looked at him and saw a pathetic man who preys on young girls trying to be nice to me. "How's your wife and daughter doing with you over here?" He gaped at me in shock. I put my foot in it by saying "and daughter" a momentary lapse of concentration, and I could have given my whole game away!

"My wife is happy to get rid of me for a few weeks. I've only got the one daughter, and she's out with your mum."

"Yeah, I know. I just meant your wife."

"Okay. I'm heading out for a run. Good luck with your work. I hope I can get to use the sauna before we leave." He slithered out, taking a banana from the fruit bowl.

Just being in his presence made me angry. I had to keep him away from Rae. She probably didn't even know that she was been kidnapped. She probably thought it's normal to run away with some old guy and stay in hiding, lying to everyone they meet! To even come up with this idea, Barry must be some sort of psychopath. How did he even approach convincing her to leave home and go to the other side of the world? How did she agree with it? She must have been desperate.

Back in my room, I went looking into Barry's life. The problem with him was his age; people over 40 didn't really have much of a social media presence. He had a Facebook and a LinkedIn account that bored me to tears. He was a corporate drone. The people he was connected to looked like stock photos for 'generic office people'.

I was left with some tough choices to make, but most of all, I had to get the facts right. I needed to speak to Rae one on one and see what the hell was going on.

Everyone was out, so I went down the garden and started digging small trenches leading from the back of the house down to the shed for the electric cables, but the rain was making it very messy. Every noise I heard sounded like a car pulling up to the house or the front door opening. I was jumpy, but at least I wasn't feeling sick anymore. That brief encounter with Barry made me feel better for some reason. I felt like I could compete with him. I already knew I was cleverer than him but just seeing how lame he gave me the belief that I could snatch Rae away from him.

I wanted to get discovered working in the rain, I thought it would look dramatic and suit the situation, but I gave up before everyone got home. No point making myself ill.

Mum and Rae eventually came home when I was in the upstairs toilet. I stayed in there. Barry was in the house again now, downstairs watching TV. I could hear them all in the living room talking, but it was muffled. Footsteps made their way up the stairs and into my bedroom - Rae's temporary room. I went and knocked on her door.

"Come in."

"Hey," I said as I opened the door.

"Hey." She was unpacking a bag from Topshop onto the bed. Even then, it was clear she was ignoring the elephant in the room. Maybe that's how she handles everything, just ignore it, and it'll go away. I don't operate that way. I stepped into the room and closed the door behind me.

"We need to talk about what's going on."

She stopped what she was doing and sat on the side of the bed.

"It's complicated, isn't it?" She said, still facing the other way.

"Who knows you're here?" I don't know why this was my opening question because I didn't actually care who knew she was here. Mostly I wanted to know what the hell she was doing with Barry!

"My parents think I'm on holiday with some friends."

Right then, my mum called up, wanting me to come down. It seemed like this wasn't the time to get to the truth. I needed an opportunity where no one was around.

I went down to my mum, who was acting more relaxed. "How was your day?" She walked round to close the door as she spoke.

"Really productive, thanks. How was yours?"

When the door was closed, she whispered, "That is a very strange girl!" Now that I knew my mum wasn't crazy in thinking something was wrong, I found it very difficult to disagree with her. "She barely said a word all day. What have you gotten out of her?"

"Not much. As you say, she's quite odd."

"Has she spoken about her mum at all? Somethings definitely happening with her and Barry. I bet they are getting a divorce, and this is father-daughter time before it's over."

"Wouldn't Barry have said something to Dad if he was having trouble with his marriage?"

"That would be the normal thing to do, but Barry has always kept secrets and is a pathological liar." Without knowing it, mum had said something that was right in line with what I wanted to delve into.

"Like what? What secrets has he got?"

As mum poured a glass of wine for herself, she clearly sensed I was keen to find gossip out, so she took her time and lapped up the spotlight. "Do you want some dinner?"

"Mum! Tell me about Barry. I want to know."

She smiled and got comfortable at the kitchen table. I sat opposite her.

"I only knew Barry for a couple of years before he left, but your dad and him hung out with each other all the time when we began seeing each other. He was around 23, and I was 19 or 20. There was nothing strange about your dad. He was who he is now, sporty and always lots of fun." How he ever got my mum to fall for him will forever be the greatest mystery to me. She still talked about him like he was some football hunk. He was a mess, for christ sake, same as now. "Barry, however, was very friendly but twitchy. Do you know what I mean?"

"Twitchy? How?"

"He never held eye contact or held a conversation well."

"What about his secrets?" AKA, get to the point, mum!

"Just some of the things David used to tell me about him made it clear he was hiding something. I knew for sure that he used prostitutes here and there as well as the fact he slept with a lot of very unattractive women. Even though he wasn't bad looking. In fact, there were girls I knew who really fancied him. He just preferred the one night stands with the drunkest women in the bar and also hookers."

"Dad told you this?"

"He did, but also people in our group of friends spoke about him. When he had girlfriends, no one ever met them. And he was arrested under strange circumstances before he left for Australia."

JACKPOT! "What circumstances?"

She leaned into me. "The police pulled him over for speeding, and they saw all over the back seat were bags of women clothes. When he was asked about it, he drove off. They chased him and arrested him, but nothing ever came of it."

"That's weird." I was stumped. What did it mean?

She nodded. "Your dad said the same as he did. He was just running the bags down the charity shop for someone, but we never knew who because none of us knew his girlfriends. I thought that they might have just been his collection of women clothes he kept over the years, you know, like trophies or something gross, but your dad never wanted to talk about it."

"And you let him stay here?"

"That was nearly 20 years ago, and he's always been fine, really. He brought his daughter with him, which I just had to see." She sipped wine. "I couldn't imagine what sort of relationship he'd have with a daughter. Now I've seen that she's strange; it all makes sense."

Barry sounded totally unhinged. What the fuck was mum thinking? She's safe up in bed with Del, but no thought went into Barry, the weirdo, being in the house with their young son? What was all that about the women clothes in the car? He could have just murdered someone and got caught ditching the evidence.

Mum finished her glass of wine. "Maybe I shouldn't be so suspicious of Lucy when Barry is her dad. Not her fault she's strange." Just then, Del came in through the kitchen door.

"Whats strange?" He said clearly overhearing the tail end of the chat.

"Barry." That's all my mum said and got up to kiss him.

"Oh yeah. Sure, but top bloke."

I had to get more ammunition than this if I was going to take Barry down. This could be something that Del could be useful for. "Whats going on with the sauna? Looks like a spaceship."

"The metal is to insulate it." I didn't know how I would get anything out of Del. Even that brief exchange managed to annoy me. Before it went any further, I left and went into my room/the dining room. Barry was still on the sofa, but at least I knew where he was. I was going to have to monitor him closely.

15

I could imagine making it work with Rae now she wasn't not Lucy, but for her sake, I had to focus on getting information from her on the exact nature of her relationship with Barry. Before I could attempt to help her, I needed to know the facts.

Occasionally horrible thoughts of what they might be doing on their day trips made my guts twist. I read up on a story of a teacher who left the country with his 15-year-old student in 2012. They fled so they could have sex because it was legal in France. So technically, he wasn't a paedo there... technically. If being a paedo was judged on margins as thin as what the French are ok with, then in my opinion, you're still a paedo. The police would also agree.

Still, if I was to get Rae to like me, I couldn't get the police involved straight away, but I didn't have long to sort it out. I had no idea of their schedule. Barry might have been sorting a place for them to stay. To me, it looked like he spent most of his time on the sofa or going to random places, probably just as a cover.

I had to pick up parts for The CryoShed. I didn't want to start the deep freeze by laying on just a hard metal shell so some memory foam was going to line the inside of the 'capsule' / the tank I was due to collect from the metal yard. A quick google search found a place that sold thin memory foam in Hammersmith, which wasn't easy to get to from where I was. It would take a couple of hours there and back, so plenty of time to dig deep into what's going on. I invited Rae to come with me that morning. She didn't look totally enthused, but it was either come with me or stay at the house all day. Barry had already left to do whatever creeps do during the daytime. Probably sit in a park reading yesterdays newspaper, gawping at women as they jog.

On the train, I told her that we were picking memory foam for the sauna. She bought the lie. To get answers out of her, I had to be sneaky. I started by talking about the other night and saying it was fun. Getting drunk and talking. She was laughing about some of the people that were there. Apart from that initial shock they were in from seeing me with a girl, they were no more strange than usual.

Asking about Rae's life was awkward. She had been lying so much over the past few weeks that I bet she almost forgot what the truth even was. Before I left that morning, I watched a YouTube video on 'How To Tell If Someone's Lying to You" by a woman who used to be in the CIA. It wasn't the physical 'tells' like scratching the nose, wiggling feet or crossing arms that were the give aways. It was behaviour like being defensive and talking a lot while not answering the question. If you get those kinds of responses with the physical 'tells,' the likelihood is that the subject is lying. With this new CIA knowledge, I began the interrogation on the southeast overground from Ashcave to Waterloo. My technique was to make it conversational and casual. First of all, I spoke about school. This line of questioning was designed to see how old she really was.

"This year, we were supposed to have exams, but they got cancelled. They're designed to help you choose what to do in the next couple of years leading up to Uni. Did you have exams this year?" I asked, watching her mannerisms intently, but because we had to wear a mask on all public transport, it was quite hard to tell what sort of face she was making.

"Yeah, but I'm not in school much." She replied as casually as ever.

"Yeah, me neither. Just every day." I said, forcing a bit of a bizarre laugh.

I think she smiled back. "How did they grade you with no exams?"

"They used predictions based on your past work, which has stitched me up because I didn't do any work for the last few months of school. I was relying on acing the tests." My probing was laboured and slow; I had to be more direct. "Are you going into sixth form?"

"I don't think we have the same system as you do." Maybe she saw right through my line of questioning as an obvious bout of information digging.

I blurted out. "How old are you?" My patience had run out before the second stop of the train journey. She was looking out the window. I could see her eyes look towards me without turning her head. She had caught onto what I'm doing here.

"It's my birthday in 2 weeks." That's not an answer.

"Cool. You'll be here then. How old will you be?"

"16," She said, finally giving me the information I was after.

Even though I always questioned the fact that she might be 15, I honestly thought she was older. I hoped that the fake ID she used was her real one and that she was just lying about who she was. I couldn't figure out why, though. She was tall and older looking than my friends and me. Deep down, I really thought she was older. The fact that she was the same age as me and had fled her home with an old man was real. My wild imagination making this gross situation as bad as possible was actually right. She was underage and having a relationship with an old married man. I wondered how she could do this? I sat for a little bit, thinking of my line of inquiry.

"How did you end up coming over here with Barry?"

"It's a long story." She said, looking out the window and offering nothing further.

I couldn't get the words out to ask more about it. I'm not used to grilling someone about their life. If it were reversed, I wouldn't say anything either. What business was it of mine?

We got into Hammersmith and bought what I needed. A rolled-up thin memory foam, and again we were carrying something too big for one person.

Stopping for lunch before we got on the train, I felt we had a better opportunity to talk, even if the vibe was still stiff. I didn't help matters there, though. I hadn't loosened up an inch all day. Physically I was constricted around her all the time. Clenching my bum and stomach in case she was looking at me.

She seemed to chill a bit while we ate. I felt anxious about everything and in need of some answers but felt like I wasn't going to get any. While we ate falafel wraps in a little kebab shop near the station, we spoke about London being crowded, and I mentioned how many pubs there were everywhere, "More than any other city apparently...".

She told me about her job working in a hotel in Sydney. It turned out hotels in Australia aren't like hotels here. They were bars and casinos as well. She worked collecting glasses, a job set up by her mum, who knew the owner. That's where she met Barry. That's all the information I got out of her. I temporarily filled in the blanks. We made our way back home, and she didn't really mention anything else about what was going on with her and Barry.

The times we had gone out together, she hadn't spent much time on her phone, but as it got later in the day, whenever we got somewhere with WiFi, she was texting on it constantly. I didn't know who she was messaging, but she seemed exasperated with every message received.

Now I knew a little bit more about her, I felt more of a responsibility to help her. The main problem was that the whole summers plan could get torn apart by the mayhem. If the police and media got involved, that would be even more reason to escape the situation. I felt like I was deeply selfish thinking on these terms. As far as I could tell, Rae had been honest with me. I didn't pick up on any of the tells that I learned from the CIA video that morning. It was actually very hard to pick up on things like that when listening to what's being said. I'll be able to practice this at home on Del. He's a liar, so I'll just need to ask him what he had for breakfast for the lies to fall out of his mouth.

When we got back home, mum was acting very strange with me raising her eyebrows at Rae when she wasn't looking. She clearly thought things were getting pally between me and 'Lucy'. I didn't think that we were friends but we did have something connecting us, a secret.

Back on the inflatable mattress, I looked at the Sydney news to see if anything had been mentioned. Nothing in the local press as far as I could see. I googled Rae's name again, and up came news story and video from a national newspaper website!

16

Rae's mum had written to a news channel saying her daughter had left the country with someone they don't know. They have had minimal contact with her. The video on the news channel showed an old woman. She looked too old to have a daughter as young as Rae. She was shaking as she spoke. I thought that she was clearly very upset. She didn't say where her daughter had gone. Obviously, they now knew that she's not away with a friend on holiday.

Rae probably knew this was coming. I had made many assumptions about what's going on, one of them being that she had at least made sure her parents knew she was alive. This proved to be true because this was a report that Rae had left the country, not that she had vanished without a trace.

The video was a huge revelation. How long would it take for people over there to join the dots, and for Barry to get picked up as the person who's effectively kidnapped her? Pressure to do something on my end had been increased exponentially!

When the house was asleep at around 1 am, I went up to my room to speak to Rae. I could see from the blue light leaking out underneath the door that she was up. I went in, and she was in the dark on her phone, wide awake. I had my laptop on me, wanting to show her the video. I stood at the end of the bed. I didn't need to say anything. She launched into one.

Trying to control her volume with a hushed tone, she said, "My mum went on the news to talk about me. I can never ever go back now. She went to the fucking news! I've been telling her that I'm fine and staying with a family. I've not told her where or who with because she'd freak out, but she freaked out anyway! Who goes to the news with private family stuff? She will love this attention. You can see why I left now!"

Not really, I was thinking. It looked like she was just desperate to get her child back home safely, but something between Rae and her mum must have been going on. I let her rant for a while longer. This turned out to be the best way to get information out of her.

Rae's mum was an alcoholic and, by Rae's account, a bad one. Not violent, but just very moody. She would fall over a lot and make things very uncomfortable whenever anyone was around. This caused the relationship with her husband to be stretched. He was very distant and never engaged emotionally. Eventually he had an affair but never left the house. Her mum forgave him but never let anyone forget, bringing up the affair at every opportunity. He just took it and shut up. Rae said he was more interested in his guns than either of them.

She had wanted to run away for a long time. Barry came into her life and was unlike both of her parents and seemed like a better option than a guy her own age. She spoke about him like a saviour; mature, sensitive, worldly, interesting and intelligent... He was NONE of these things. She must have been in a dark place, like a black hole where no light could reach her, AT ALL, to see these qualities in Barry. What were the other guys like around her for her to see this, for christ sake?

She began crying after I said I had found the video and that people would start to put what was going on together. I thought I was making some ground until I said that Barry was kidnapping her and that he'd be seen as a paedophile by the police. She lurched up at me. "We've not even had sex, so how could he be?!"

I had gotten all the information I needed to sleep that night. She clearly thought she was in love with Barry, and I guess he must have been in love with her to leave his family. I still thought he was a paedo for even being with her like this, but the fact that they hadn't had sex made me feel slightly better. What were they thinking leaving the country together? I left her after the rant. I think it tired her out, I checked for the blue light under the door, and the phone didn't go back on when I left.

17

The last major thing I needed for The Cryoshed was liquid nitrogen, but no one would sell me any, legally. Over a few weeks, I contacted various companies to acquire what I needed, but the hoops I had to jump through were ridiculous. I had to have proof of correct storage conditions, show my company details, be over 21, pay by bank transfer and wait a month for delivery. I was storing it in a shed; I had no company, was 15, wanted to pay with cash, and I wanted it now.

I was forced into making inquiries in areas of the internet that I wasn't 100% comfortable with, but you have to take some risk in life to achieve greatness. I watched some YouTube tutorials on how to use the dark web and found a site where I could log into a forum and ask about the availability of Liquid Nitrogen in London. I got a response a few hours after posted it from a user called 'KingFlippyNips'. - Hi IceBoy2120 (my username). I have what you need and can arrange a cash exchange and pick up. Go to private chat, and we can organise.

So KingFlippyNips and I spoke in a private chat, exchanged numbers and organised a price. £1300 for one gallon of liquid nitrogen. This was over the price others were charging, but the convenience came at a cost.

This meant I had one more trip to make into London. KingFlippyNips wanted to meet somewhere quiet where there weren't too many CCTV cameras or tourists. I said that I was coming on the train from the south, so he suggested a place near Waterloo station near some arches. I agreed and told him I'd be in touch when I can get a train. I had almost all of my boxes ticked now, so it was a matter of days till The CryoShed was completed.

It was the day after Rae's rant and Del was milling about down by the shed for the first time this summer. I was watching him from inside the house. He was on the phone arguing with someone, but he was lowering his voice, so I couldn't hear what it about. Then there were lots of sharp movements like he was really having a go at someone then it seemed the tone changed, and he looked like he was apologising.

As his conversation finished, he looked upset. When he hung up, he got closer to the shed started to inspect my workmanship, like he knew what he was doing. Tapping the metal where I soldered pieces together and looking at the heavy-duty door hinges I put on. To me, it looked like my project was starting to take shape, at least from the outside. Inside it looked a bit budget. Just large rolls of memory foam, insulation and tin foil. The insulation and memory foam were easy to explain, but the tin foil didn't make much sense for a sauna. I walked down to interrupt before he started messing with things.

"Looks like you've really gone to town on the sauna." He said as I approached.

"Yeah, but it's not done yet, so don't touch anything. Who was on the phone?" He looked down at me and took a step back, putting his phone in his pocket.

"No one, just work.' He paused and looked back at the shed. 'It's very different to other saunas I've seen. More metal."

"Yeah, it's a new design. I've taken a more modern German approach rather than the traditional Scandinavian." I made that up completely on the spot, but he nodded along with it.

"You know, if you need some help finishing it off, I'd love to help."

He would want to get involved as it was nearly done and claim the glory. "Thanks, but I'm on top of it. Should be done soon." He shrugged and nodded, walking back up towards the house.

Just before he went inside, he called back at me, "It looks, great Son." Clearly, something was going on with him. He never showed interest in me or called me 'Son'.

I had to ramp things up. I was already past my completion date target. The distraction of Rae had affected me. I couldn't completely blame her, though. Getting hold of the parts hadn't been as simple as I'd hoped. That would get rectified once I get the liquid nitrogen.

That weekend the house was full, and it was very hard to escape into London on my own. Mum had recently decided to start writing a blog. It was her 'Covid Project'. She wanted to reconnect with some science interests, and she thought writing about what she was learning as she was learning it would help motivate her. She said my building work inspired her. I was actually quite interested in seeing what type of stuff would interest her in the modern world. When she was at University, there was no Large Hadron Collider, Hubble telescope or even the internet really. She could learn just about anything now. I was happy she had decided to do this.

Del was in the living room talking to Barry. When I passed them, they were talking about plans for the next couple of days. Barry looked stressed as Del just rabbited on. The plans sounded as boring as you'd expect. I went up to see Rae. I knocked and went in when given permission.

"Hey. How's it going?" Rae was sitting up on the bed with her phone in her hand, looking at me as I walked in.

"Did you say something to Barry?" She asked.

"About what?" I went in and closed the door.

"You know."

"I've not said anything to anyone. I want to, though."

"You can't say anything. I trust you. So please don't."

"Okay, I won't. What's going on?"

"Barry isn't speaking to me. I think something is going on back home with his wife. He told me that he said he's leaving her, but she's ringing him, and they're talking to each other a lot. I don't know what's going on. I'm starting to think that he lied to me and that his wife thinks he's over here for work and coming back. What if that was happening and he wanted to go back?"

"Honestly, Rae, I think that's best-case scenario for you right now, but it doesn't make sense. He doesn't have to go back. He's from here and can just stay. Even if they got a divorce, he wouldn't have to go back, I don't think." I didn't have a clue what I was talking about, but this sounded right.

"What about seeing his daughter?"

I was so busy thinking about him being a disgusting creep that I forgot the lies he'd been telling my family about Rae being his daughter. That made everything so much more messed up.

"Did you know his daughter? Lucy?"

"I knew of her. Never met her. I looked at her Facebook profile, but that's it. And I've got her passport." She said, shrugging it off.

"What about his wife?" I asked.

"I looked her up quite a bit. From what Barry told me, she was pretty horrible." Of course, he would say that, I thought to myself.

"How so?"

"When we first started spending time together, he would tell me about how she changed over the years to always being angry at him. Criticising and being hurtful. He was providing for her and their daughter, but she was just mean to him." She said this as though she was reading from a script. Personally, I didn't believe anything he said to anyone.

"Do you think Barry was just telling this stuff because he fancied you?" I asked gently.

"He showed me texts from her when she was running him down."

"Any more news of what's going on back home?" I asked changing the subject slightly.

"She's got the police messaging me asking where I am. I can't turn my phone on without being harassed."

"Have you told Barry this?"

"No. He'll freak out. I just want to start a new life. I hate my life!"

Rae threw herself into the pillows and wept. This didn't feel like a show. She was crying hard. I went to give her a hug, and she held on to me. Again I could feel her tears drip onto my skin, but this time, I was only thinking about how to get in contact with the police in Australia. I couldn't let this go on. It could end up getting the whole family in trouble with the police.

My plan for the day was to get out of the house, but that was quashed as soon as I went downstairs. Del was with mum in the kitchen.

"Get your coat on. We're all going out." He proclaimed.

"I don't feel like it, to be honest."

Mum chimed in, "Come on it's a lovely day, I've booked a table for us at Blue Anchor for a pub lunch" Then she called up to Rae "Lucy, want to come for some lunch, Darling?" Then she smiled at me like she was doing me a favour. Rae opened the door and came downstairs completely up for it.

I couldn't understand the way she worked. One minute she's balling with tears, then suddenly she's chipper and wants to go out for lunch with everyone? I couldn't say no now. Part of me was curious to see Barry and Rae together. I hadn't spent any time with the two of them together since I'd found out their secret. I grabbed a jacket and got in the car with everyone. Rae sat in between my mum and me. The awkwardness of the trip was set up well by Del randomly asking Lucy/Rae if she had a boyfriend. Her shake of the head cued up an awkward silence that lasted the drive to the pub.

The Blue Anchor was the pub we went to when mum and dad wanted a nice meal. It was a gastro pub where you could see the kitchen through a big hole in the wall. It had been done up a few years ago, but most of the furniture was pretty old. The main building was very old, like hundreds of years old. The floor had these heavy-looking slate panels that had a shine on them from so many thousands of footsteps walking on them. I said to Rae that this pub was older than her country, as a joke. She didn't respond.

It was overcast but not cold, so we went and sat outside on a long wooden bench. The pub garden was packed with mostly families, no more than six to a table as were the rules of Covid. When we got to the table, a couple of blokes were down one end drinking pints. They wouldn't leave, and Del had to show his alpha male strength, but neither of them was even remotely scared. The waitress eventually asked them to move.

I sat opposite Rea, and Barry was next to me. I tried not to brush elbows with him. Sitting next to him made my skin crawl enough, without touching him as well.

Del calmed down a bit when the trey of drinks arrived and decided that the main topic of conversation should be what I've done to the garden shed. Del used it as an opportunity to have a laugh with Barry about what a sauna should look like, and that mine looks nothing like a sauna. They took turns saying what it did look like making my mum laugh;

Del "A space ship."

Barry "A micro prison."

Del "A robots shit."

Barry "Robocops dogs house."

This went on for a while until Rae blurted out, "A cryogenic freezing lab". I looked at her straight away. She looked down her nose at her bottle of Appletizer and sucked the straw. Everyone around the table laughed briefly before moving onto a different subject.

I was stunned.

It felt like I was burning up as nervousness filled my entire body. I was sat paralysed with it.

Did she know what I was up to, or was that some insanely ridiculous guess? If she knew, how did she know? I've been moving around the blueprints to different storage places on a daily basis and never seen them disturbed. If she knew, why hadn't she asked me about it? I left the table and went to the toilet. I sat in the cubicle and sweated. I ignored the smell of piss mixed with urinal cakes and the graffiti telling me to 'call this number for a toothy BJ'. My fear was that Rae might now have some leverage over me. I couldn't say anything to anyone about what she's up to because she would just tell everyone about what I'm planning. The success of the mission completely depends on its secrecy. If my parents knew I was effectively running away from them forever, they would smash the shed to pieces.

It took about 10 minutes to bring my pulse down.

I went back to the table, and Del commented on how long I was in there, implying that I had been either shitting or wanking. I'm sure I looked sick, so cla ming ill health was easy. I coughed a couple of times, and that sent everyone within ear shot into a minor panic, so Mum took me back home and left everyone else in the pub. Once she dropped me off, she went back to join them. I had to find out what Rae knew.

Up in her temporary accommodation, I started lifting the mattress and going through her things. She really did pack light before leaving Australia. She didn't have a diary like I was hoping. No photos either. Everything is online now, so no surprise there, really. Her personal belongings didn't extend much further than a phone charger and wrappers for Australian chocolate bars stuffed in the pockets of her ruck sack.

I went back down to my temporary room to see if my things have been disturbed recently. I had just changed the hiding place from the back of the sofa to the most recent hiding place, the posh cutlery box. This cutlery box was wooden on the outside; the knives and forks were placed in lines moulded into a plastic fixing that looked like it was felt; it was actually cheap plastic and could be pulled off as a whole, leaving a space behind it with a couple of centimetres storage. We never used that cutlery, and there was no way Rae would think to look in there for any reason. The papers were fine. Undisturbed.

Now I had to contemplate that it was a wild guess? What if she just looked at what was in the garden and thought - It looks like he's building a shelter to freeze himself in. That would be an astonishingly observant thought. I knew what I was creating, yet I knew it didn't look like any lab or chamber created before. It was a homemade version of something that would cost millions. All this was going through my mind when everyone came home. I got into bed, put Netflix on my laptop and tried to look sick. Del came to the door to see me.

"You alright, Paddy?"

"Yeah, I'll be fine, thanks." He nodded then shouted out to Barry,

"Better not come in here. It smells like he's really ill, haha" Then he closed the door and left. He literally only came in to take the piss out of me. I really had to speed up my work to get the hell away from here!

THE BLUEPRINTS

Patrick Walters - Cryoshed Blueprints 01

June 2020

To get:

- Air con unit / air cooler tsc
- Cryo pod (large cylinder)
  e.g. industrial oven type thing?
  fridge?
  boiler? — must be 6ft +
- Insulation
- Industrial rolls of tin foil
- Liquid nitrogen (enough for 100 years)
- Memory foam for pod
- Roofing
- Scrap metal sheets
- Piping
- Insulated electronic cables

Initial sketches

Birds eye view

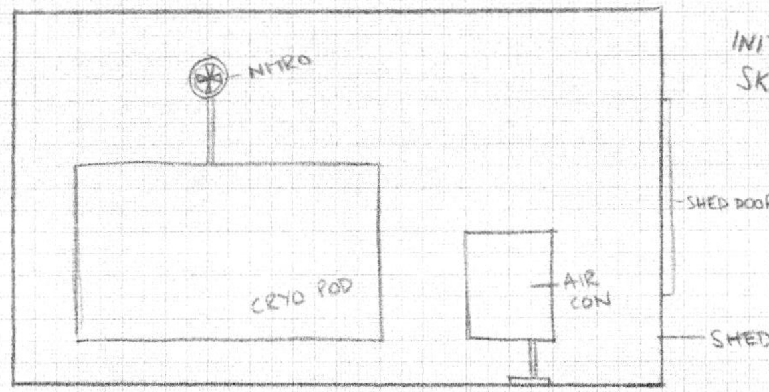

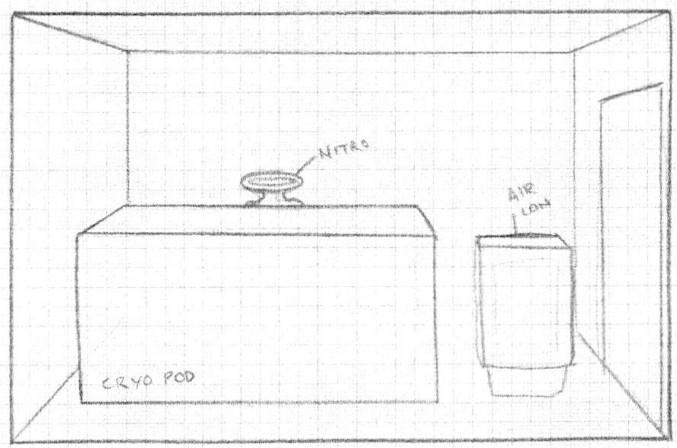

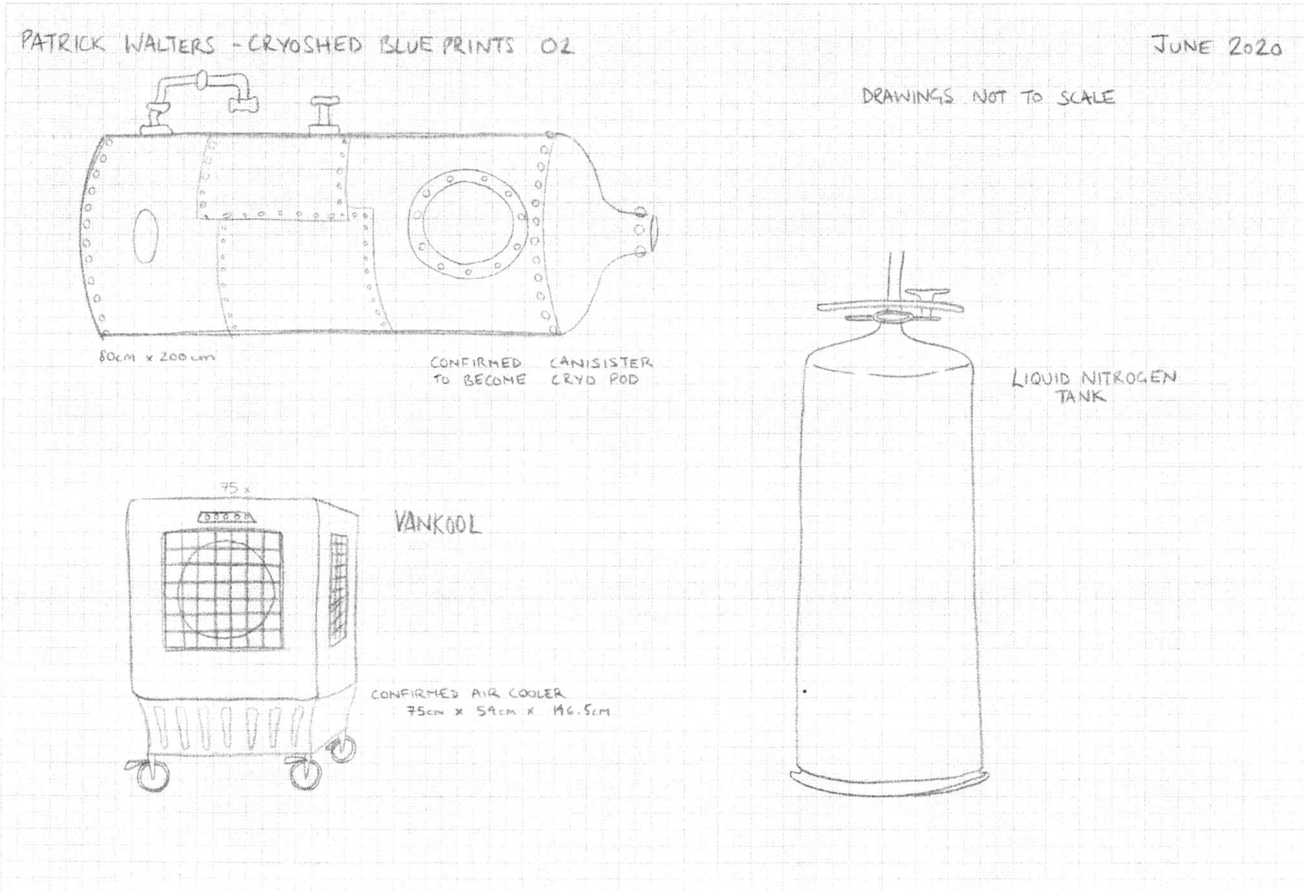
PATRICK WALTERS - CRYOSHED BLUE PRINTS 02
JUNE 2020
DRAWINGS NOT TO SCALE
80cm x 200cm
CONFIRMED CANISISTER
TO BECOME CRYO POD
LIQUID NITROGEN
TANK
75 x
VANKOOL
CONFIRMED AIR COOLER
75cm x 54cm x 146.5cm

PATRICK WALTERS - CRYO SHED BLUEPRINTS 02

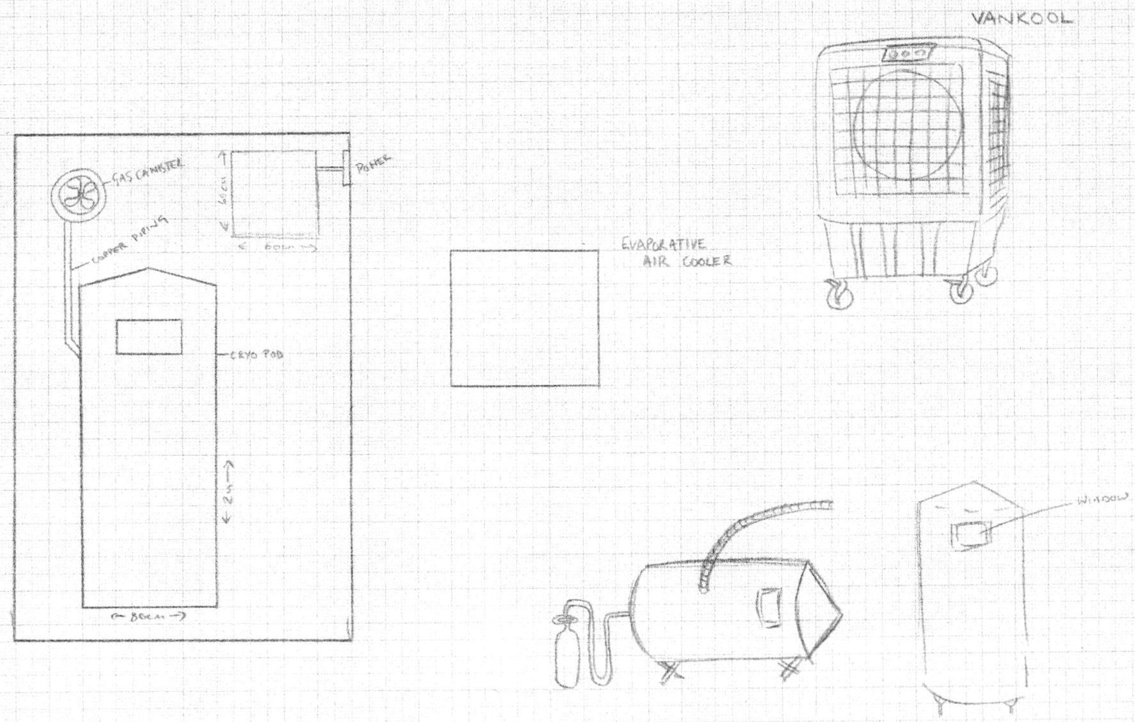

PATRICK WALTERS - CRYOSHED BLUEPRINTS 03

JUNE 2020

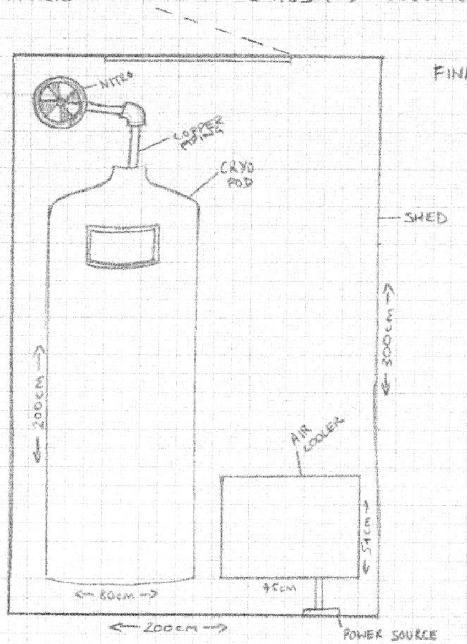

FINAL BIRDS EYE VIEW

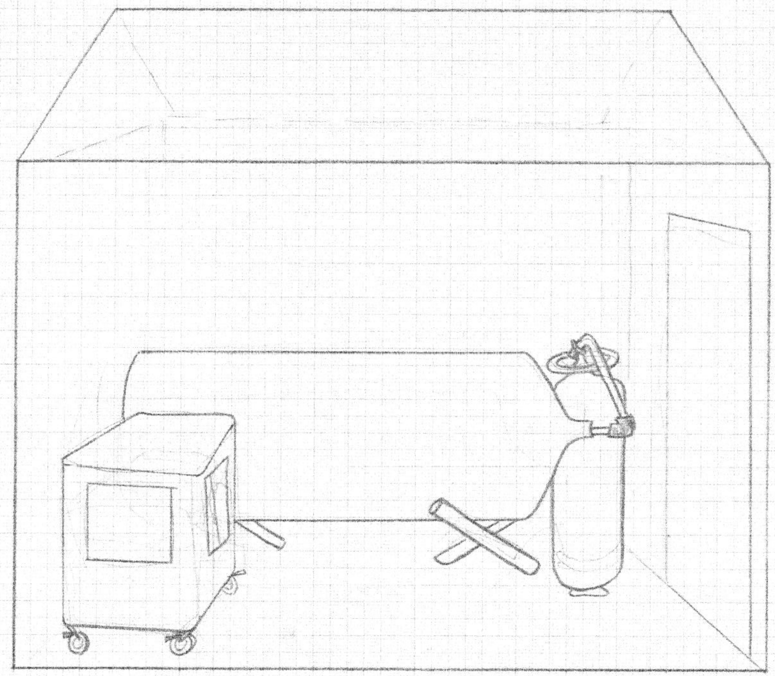

18

Rae was a different person from minute to minute. I couldn't keep up. When I thought she was upset, she'd be fine 5 minutes later. When I thought I understood her, she threw something at me out of the blue, just like at lunch. I stayed in hiding for the rest of the day. Playing sick kept me out of doing things with everyone. I was knackered anyway.

My sleeping pattern was a mess. Not only was there the fear of someone knowing my plan to freeze myself for 100 years, but I was also getting seriously bored of sleeping on a blow-up bed. It either had a tiny hole in it somewhere, or the cap on it wasn't completely air tight. Before I went to sleep, I pumped it up to bursting point only to wake up with my face on the hard floor and the mattress half-wrapped around me. No one would argue with the idea of escaping to an entirely new time when I explained the situation I was in.

Rea and Barry had been at the house for three weeks now. I had two weeks to finish The Cryoshed before school started up again. There's no way I was going back to school. I wasn't sure if they would even put me in the same year group because I did such little work last year. My parents received a letter from my school instructing them to forward my grades from summer school when they come through. I knew because I'd been intercepting all post just in case this happened. Obviously, I didn't enrol on an online summer school! I didn't deliver the letter that said I had to go in the first place. Going back to school was not an option!

The goals for today were to buy a lock to keep people out while I make the final touches to the shed and to go into London to buy the Liquid nitrogen. The next day I had to pick up the hibernation chamber from the scrap yard.

All this was extremely important and needed to be taken care of, but I needed to know what Rae knew before even thinking about getting back to work.

I was in the kitchen in what I thought was an empty house because there were no cars in the driveway. I did my whole morning routine without seeing anyone. But Rae slunk downstairs without me hearing.

Just a couple of casual "Hey"'s from each of us, to begin with. I had to broach the subject subtly. If I just came out with you saying my shed looks like a cryogenic freezing lab was funny, what made you say that, it would be too blatant. Tact was key here.

I opened with, "Did you have fun at lunch yesterday?"

"Not really. Your dad can be a bit much sometimes."

"Yeah I know." Christ I knew. This was a good opening for me though. "When he said the sauna looks like a robots shit it kind of summed up his imagination" Rae stuck some bread in the toaster and looked down into the mouth of it while it heated up, saying nothing. I was relying on her engaging in the conversation for this to work. "Then Barry with the Robocops dog house?" Still nothing from her. "And then you with the, what did you say? Cryo something lab?"

She sighed and turned to face me. "Look, Patrick. I know what you're trying to build in the shed. I've not said anything because I kind of didn't believe you'd actually try to build it."

"W..." She cut me off.

"I had a root around your bedroom when I first got here." She admitted.

I was stunned. Rae knew about The CryoShed! She hadn't said anything because she'd simply dismissed it?

"You went through my stuff? That's a huge invasion of privacy. I'm very upset." I wasn't. She shrugged her shoulders. "And you don't think I'll be able to build it?"

"What are you more bothered by? Me being nosy? Or not thinking you're capable of building something like this? And by the way, I was jet-lagged with nothing to do, so what was I supposed to do in the middle of the night apart from having a nose through your stuff?"

The toast popped out, and she started assembling her breakfast like all of this was no big deal.

"I really don't want anyone finding out what I'm doing."

"You're not doing a very good job of making it unsuspicious. There's no way that looks like a sauna. Couldn't you come up with another cover story? Like a science project for school?"

That was a fair point in hindsight. The shed had taken on the size and look of something... That something not being a sauna. "But I won't tell anyone what you're doing." She finally said.

"Well, you did yesterday," I said, trying to get back on the front foot.

"Sorry. I won't say anything again. What are you even building it for? To be honest, I only saw the drawing of the inside chamber. I didn't look much at the rest."

"Blueprints."

"What?"

"They're not called drawings. They're called blueprints."

"Okay, blueprints, sorry. Why are you trying to build it?"

I weighed up my options with Rae. Everything that was going on in her life was so dramatic. Anything I told her about my life would seem so boring and insignificant. So I lied. "I just want to see if I can freeze an animal and bring it back to life." That sounded less strange in my head. She looked at me with a kind of confused horror.

"Pads, that's kind of sick. What type of animal?"

"I haven't chosen one yet." This was sounding worse and worse as the words left my mouth. In her head, this had gone from me building an experiment to building some mad animal torture chamber. She picked up her plate and walked towards the door. I had screwed this up royally very quickly. "Wait. Okay, it's not for animals. It's for me. I'm building a freezing chamber to put myself in a frozen hibernation for 100 years. It's not for animals. I'm doing it to myself." She turned back around and leaned against the kitchen wall.

"Why?"

"This is going to sound stupid, but I just want to escape." She sat down and looked at me with a warmth she'd only showed me once before, the time when she was drunk just before telling me about her and Barry.

"I can understand that. But why? Everything's nice here."

"Yeah that's how you see it. For me I've been stuck in this house with a dad that basically hates me and makes my life difficult at every opportunity. He takes the piss out of me and is such an imbecile he's incapable of having a proper conversation. You've heard him. That's half of it. He gave up being nice to me when I was about 6, and it was obvious I wasn't going to play sports. I remember when it was." I was in a flow here and had Rae fully focused. "We were in a field nearby where we lived. It was around the time when school tryouts for the football team were on. I wanted to be in the team to make him happy. But I had no chance. I was smaller than everyone else and had no coordination. He took a football with us to the park and tried to teach me how to kick it. I couldn't even manage kicking it from my hands. He said to drop it onto my foot as I swung it up to kick, but I kept throwing it up before I kicked it. I know now what the problem was, but he had no patience. He quit trying to teach me and gave up. When I didn't get on the football team, he was ashamed. I knew then I couldn't go to him for anything anymore. I know my mum loves me, but she never tries to help me out with him and would be happier if she didn't have to think about me at all. And, I hate school. It's literally a prison where they force you to learn facts for tests that will be irrelevant in the next 10 years, in amongst hormonal guys always trying to impress each other by doing something more stupid than the next person, usually at someone else's expense. It's a cruel place to be, but it's the only place to get away from this house." Saying all this in one go was tiring.

"Okay, maybe it's not that nice here." She said

when I finally took a breath.

I was shocked by my rant, but at least I'd opened up to Rae about reasoning. "I need to get this built and me froze before school starts back in two weeks. I can't go back."

"Isn't it dangerous?"

She was concerned for my safety. Above all, that felt good! I explained the rest of the plan, telling her everything. She promised not to reveal the plan to anyone and even offered to help finish the construction with me. I took her down to the shed and showed her exactly what I was doing.

I figured that having an extra pair of hands would be very useful in finishing on time. She was fascinated by the work I had done and the little details I was putting in. It dawned on me that we had this want to find something new and start again in common. We were just going about it completely differently. I thought what she was doing was insane and dangerous. She thought the exact same about what I was doing. She was helping me. I wanted to help her, but how? Mostly I wanted to protect her from Barry.

We made a plan to walk to the station, so I text KingFlippyNips, and we decided to meet near Waterloo station to do the exchange, so I didn't have to walk too far with the canister. He was pissed off with me for leaving him hanging the last time, but I promised that I was 100% getting it this time because I needed it urgently.

Before we went, I checked online, looking for examples of girls running away with older men to see how they turned out. I'd done this before, but I wanted to be armed with some facts to try and put her off. Rae was more mature than me. I knew that. But I was convinced she wasn't mature enough to make a life here with an old man. Things for her at home must have been so bad to think Barry was a good option. I had to address that.

Rae had accepted my friend request a couple of days ago, and before we left, I went on her Facebook and looked for some of her friends who had posted on her page expressing concern for her. I wanted to know what they knew. How to do this without bringing attention to who I am was the difficult part. Police in Australia were looking for her. They'd see me asking questions and get in contact with police here. Rae's escape plan had so many more strands to it than mine, but I thought I could figure out how to help her before I went into the freeze or before she and Barry disappeared.

19

Both of us stood looking out at the Monday afternoon Waterloo station. Even though I'd been into London twice since it opened after lockdown, seeing Waterloo so quiet was eerie. It felt a little post apocalyptic.

The exits point two separate ways, so we chose to turn to the nearest.

As we left the station, I got a WhatsApp message from KingFlippyNips with a pin dropped to his location. By the looks of the pin, he was standing in the station. I messaged him to say I couldn't see him.

He replied - I'm under the station. You have to walk outside and down a ramp into the underbelly of the station.

Rae looked over my shoulder, reading the message at the same time as me, and said, "This sounds mysterious."

I said, "Yeah." but I was really thinking about how dangerous it sounded.

We follow the path from the station down round the side and see a ramp that had been blocked and not used by any kind of transport in years. There was a gap that people used to walk down, but it only looked like homeless, and possibly graffiti artists used it. There wasn't any light coming from it, so I definitely didn't want to go down. Now, this really did look like what London would look like after a zombie apocalypse.

I looked at Rae, who wore an evil grin on her face, clearly loving the element of danger this little trip has opened up. It was alright for her, she wasn't the one carrying £1300 in cash in her pockets.

I messaged KingFlippyNips again. - Can't we meet outside?

Too many cameras - was all I got back.

Fair enough. I had always guessed that this was some

stolen product, and with that text, he'd pretty much confirmed it.

I looked up from my phone. Rae was already halfway down the ramp climbing over piles of bin bags and some burned up wooden pallets to get to the hole in the fence. I jogged over, looking around to see if anyone was following us. If it wasn't midday on a Monday, I might have turned around and left, but clearly no one noticed us.

Rae went first, and I stepped into the dank and dirty abyss after her. The whiff of piss smelt like dry urine was coating the black brick walls, and the sounds of trains reverberated through the walls and filled the muggy air with trundelling sounds. Light was coming from both ends of a long tunnel. At the source of one end, I could see that beyond the curve, maybe one hundred meters down was another source. I was trying to know my exits in case we had to leg it!

I looked down for something sturdy to place my feet on and saw the path was mostly clear. Once my eyes adjusted, I saw the walls were being used as a canvas for street artists. Some were actually quite good. Rae was staring at everything with an open mouth. It was disgusting down there but also incredibly cool. I almost forgot I was there to collect the liquid nitrogen.

We walked in further and I could hear a noise coming from a particularly dark area of the tunnel ahead of us. Rae could hear it too.

"Are there dogs down here?" She asked. "I can hear some animals."

"More likely foxes" I replied.

We didn't speak to each other as we walked. The light I thought was coming from the other end wasn't the only light source. About halfway down was a stairwell leading up to the world above. The noises of animals and pipes dripping were clear now. I walked over to the stairs to see if KingFlippyNips was there, but I found something else. In the corner were two people. At first, I thought they might be homeless, but after looking at them for a couple of seconds, I thought they looked too clean. It was a man and a woman having sex. Rae and I froze and stared at them. From the brief glimpse I caught of the man's face, he looked about 50, like he could've been one of my school teachers. He was wearing a white shirt and blazer with his trousers round his ankles. The woman had her bare bum on the damp steps that had surely been used as a urinal hundreds of times. I couldn't see her clothes, but she had thick makeup on.

Rae grabbed my hand and suddenly said to them, 'Having fun?'

They both jolted and stopped. The man pulled up his trousers and ran up the stairs. As he went, he kept saying, 'Fuck off, fuck off, just fuck off!'

The woman was much more casual about it. She pulled her skirt back into place and looked at us before saying in an Australian accent, "You two shouldn't be down here."

"Where are you from?" Rae said excitedly, having randomly met a fellow Aussie.

"Wollongong originally. You?"

"Sydney, Blacktown." Rae said, smiling.

"Huh, small world." The woman smiled, revealing dark lipstick-stained teeth. She turned and walked away.

Rae turned and looked at me. I was totally stunned by everything that I had seen in the last few minutes, unable to speak. Suddenly a chill ran through me, and I shuddered. A metal scraping noise came from further up the tunnel, and I wanted to run, but Rae still had my hand. A shaky voice then called. "IceBoy2120?"

We both swung round to see a boy who looked a bit like an older me dragging the canister of liquid nitrogen.

"You KingFlippyNips?" I shouted back.

"Yeah. This is for you." He nodded down to the canister.

I was so relieved I started to laugh when we got closer to him.

'Jesus Pads it's massive.' Rae said so loudly that it echoed down the tunnel.

'It needs to be.' I said.

'What you need it for?' This guy asked.

I held off telling him for second. He was about 19 max, and he'd managed to get all this liquid nitrogen. I admired him, but I didn't trust him.

"I'm not going to tell you. How did you get this liquid nitrogen?"

He looked at me dead in the eyes right back and said, "I'm not going to tell you either."

There was a few moments of silence.

He looked around and said, "Can we wrap this up? It stinks of piss and dirty arseholes in here."

I walked the three meters to him and handed him the envelope. He opened it and quickly counted the money, then turned and walked away, leaving the canister behind.

"Lets go." I said.

"Okay Iceboy," Rae said, laughing.

20

The CryoShed was nearly finished. I had nearly all the parts, but whenever I was near Rae, I stopped thinking about everything to do with my plan and the prospect of having to go back to school. I was far more stressed out about everything going on in her life instead.

Even after the fun we'd had that day at Waterloo, she still looked weighed down by what was going on back home.

Her Facebook wall had half a dozen messages from friends asking where she was and if she was ok. She responded, saying she was fine. Not saying where she was or who she was with.

The case of the English school girl that ran away from home with her teacher was my main point of reference to understand what could happen if the police found her with Barry. It wasn't good. The police, in that case, found out because one of her friends told a parent. I thought to myself, that must have happened with Rae. She must have friends in the know back home. If I knew which one, maybe I could send an anonymous message and encourage her to say something. That way, she would get blamed for telling on Rae and not me. I didn't want Rae to get mad and reveal what I was doing with the shed. Also, it was imperative that there was a slim chance we could get together once Barry was out the way.

The task for that Tuesday was to pick up the canister from the metal yard that I was going to turn into a hibernation chamber/pod. Rae and I left in the afternoon.

As we approached the scrap yard, I saw Phil. He remained consistent. Sat in his porter cabin with The Sun newspaper, a cup of tea and polystyrene box with red sauce smeared in one corner, the sausage roll already devoured. He spoke to me but only looked at Rae. It was creepy and Rae stayed pretty close to me.

He had someone clear away the stuff around the chamber and had it brought to the front of the pile of scrap metal. I gave him £30 cash, as we had arranged, even though I'm sure it was his job to do stuff like that. Even though it was prearranged, I still felt like I had better do this quickly and get out of there before he changed his mind. We borrowed a trolly with some dodgy wheels, loaded it in and begun pulling it home. I got to inspect it properly for the first time while we were taking a break at the side of the road. Rae wasn't convinced by its condition.

"You're going to freeze yourself for 100 years in this? It's the rustiest thing I've ever seen."

"That's just cosmetic. Once I remove the exterior rust, it's going to be solid cast iron. I checked the screws. They're fine, and if they're fine, the rest will be for sure."

"You sure about that? It looks more than cosmetic, mate." She said, poking at the end with her finger as chunks of rust flaked off.

"It needs some love and care for sure," I said defensively.

I had a close look round the sides. The bottom right corner area where she was poking did look a bit thin. I didn't want her to ravage it too much before I got a chance to clean it, so I moved her round to the other end. Underneath, there was some corrosion where rain water would have collected, but I was sure a few years of rain wouldn't hurt something a solid as this. So we wheeled it and talked about what the future might be like. I was, of course, very positive about what could be expected.

"Technology will have progressed to the point where there will definitely be some kind of artificial intelligence far more intelligent than human beings, so it'll be able to problem-solve things like the cure for cancer, heart disease, self-driving cars and supersonic planes taking people around the world faster than ever before. I'll be the first completely healthy person to be cryogenically frozen, so they'll be excited to meet me. Like Walt Disney and some multi-millionaires, people who have been frozen all freeze themselves when they are either dead or dying. Once the brain dies, it's dead, and all these old millionaires are so out of touch with what's going on today they won't be very interesting to talk to." I didn't mention that I was excited by how gaming in virtual reality will probably be huge, or there might be surrogate bodies walking around. But I left out my theory about sex robots.

"But what if global warming carries on the way it is? The world is 1 degree hotter than 200 years ago, and they say that if things heat up to 2 degrees, then the worlds weather will change. Ice caps will fully melt and flood everywhere. Water will be evaporated from hot areas, and then places where it rains will get even more rain. It'll definitely flood here." She sounded like she knew her stuff, but I had also looked into this.

"I did some trouble shooting on this before I settled on using the garden shed. Where we are in Ashcave, we're 180m above sea level. That's far higher than you think. It's also mostly chalk underneath the dirt, which makes the rain pour away. And the house is on a hill. And I'm making the chamber's door water tight." I had all this covered.

"So what if when everywhere around here is flooded and people start building shelters in and around the area?"

"AI will have solved the problem of global warming before it gets out of hand like that. Already more inventions and things are getting made to halt the world from warming up." I said, trying to combat her negativity. Was Rae beginning to say stuff to deliberately annoy me, or did she really care?

"I don't know. The glaciers in Greenland have revealed black fungi in large patches of ice, meaning it's absorbing more heat rather than reflecting it, making the whole place melt quicker. Looks pretty bad for the future."

She didn't understand how science was changing the world, how AI and robots would fix things for us or how I hoped it would be.

"Well, by the time I'm hatched out of my cryogenic hibernation, the world would have seen the worse of everything if what you're predicting happens." I'll admit she had gotten a little under my skin. Earlier this week, she doubted I could even make this happen. Now she was doubting my assessment of the future. "What are you expecting about your trip into the unknown? I can tell you for sure that you're in a world of shit here. At least where I'm going, there's some hope." I may have lashed out a tiny bit, but I was right. She didn't say anything to that. She just pointed up to the entrance to my road.

I was completely wiped out after dragging the trolly with that canister in for just under 2 miles. The way it was veering around, I knew it would have been very difficult on my own, so I was lucky Rae was there. I wanted to get the canister into the shed without anyone finding out.

The house had a driveway with a slight slope down the house. Just a small one but the trolly would fly into the house if we weren't careful. Rae wanted to get a drink before embarking on the last leg, and I said that she could check if the coast was clear.

I investigated the damage to the canister some more while I waited for her to come back. It was in worse condition than I remember or worse in the areas I couldn't properly inspect when I had seen it before. Round the front where the window panel was bolted on was actually perfect. I think that's why I assumed the rest of it would be ok. The size was right, and it would be amazing for what I needed if it weren't for the crusty hole I found on the bottom, where it seemed like a large pipe would have been connected. Leaving it open to the elements had turned the surrounding area into a red, moist mess that had dried up into a crusty crater.

Rae was taking longer than I expected. The longer I waited, the more random things popped in my head like maybe she had slipped in the kitchen and banged her head and was bleeding out on the kitchen floor. But it was worse than that. She came out of the house and started walking up the hill towards me, with Barry. I stood looking at them approaching me, thinking, what the fuck is she doing?

Panicking, I thought it didn't take her long to sell me out. Then I wondered what that grin on his face was about. I swear you can tell someone's IQ by the way they smile. He never showed teeth, so when he smiled, it was just a wide grin along the bottom of his face. It was one of the most irritating things about him, apart from the kidnapping of a minor, obviously. I held up a hand as a greeting when they got closer.

Barry cheerily spouted, "Hey Patrick. I told you I'd help you if you needed me. This looks like a beast." Barry cheerily spouted.

I don't need your help with anything, ever, pal! Were the words on the tip of my tongue.

"This is the science project for your club, you're working on, right, Pads?" Rae did have a story she was selling. The least I said, the better at this point.

"Yeah, that's right. Didn't want to bother you with something silly like this." I said.

"So you need to get it round the back of the house through the gate?" Barry was so thick he just went with whatever Rae said.

"Yeah. It's going to be a steady as it goes manoeuvre."

"We'll have to be careful of the garage. Let's go then." Barry added.

Taking orders from him even as small as this was annoying. Wheeling it over to the driveway Barry and I had control of the trolly, and Rae kept hold of the canister to stop it from falling off. We got to the top of the driveway pretty easily, even though Barry was making it as awkward as physically possible and giving constant, pointless direction.

There was a lip where the new brickwork starts on the driveway.

"We're best tipping it a bit to get it over," I suggested.

"The wheels are a bit too small to tip; let's just pull

it back and give it an extra push. Just hold onto it." Barry chimed in with his genius.
I was too tired to argue. We pulled back the trolly about a foot from the lip and pushed forward together with Rae just in front. The canister took momentum on of its own, and the trolly stayed put, tipping forward. Rae jumped out the way, making her position in this venture completely obsolete. The 50kg cast iron cylinder rolled down the drive way chipping brick on the way until it clattered into the garage door, making a massive dent in the bottom. We all winced at the noise of the plywood splintering!

I looked at Barry, Rae looked at me, and Barry went to see how bad the damage was close up.

We rolled the canister back away from the hole in the door. It was pretty badly smashed in. The damage was focused at the bottom but had caused the whole door to buckle slightly. I went in and pushed the garage door button to open it up, but it looked like the impact broke the fixing by the motor. Del was going to love this; it'd give him the perfect excuse to have a go at me. I came back round to see Rae and Barry having a little argument. When I turned the corner, Barry stormed off into the house.

"He not helping anymore?" I asked, trying not to laugh.

"No. He's pissed because he thinks you pushed it deliberately hard, and I could have stopped it rolling." Rae said, shrugging her shoulders.

"Why would I want to damage my own property?" We just looked at the canister for a second. "We should get it into the garden before mum and dad get home."

With some unusual heavy lifting techniques and dropping it onto the grass a few times, making pretty significant dents on the way, we got it down and into the shed.

"We need to get our story together for what this science project is," I said, and she began laughing.

"I told Barry it was a competition to build a hibernation tank to get people through the cold winters here,"

Rae said.

"Great idea! Amazing. What competition, though? Won't he look it up to see what I'm doing?"

"Probably not. I don't think he cares." Her confidence wasn't relaxing me, but the lie was already told, so no point in worrying about it too much.

Just as we got in the back door, I heard my mum come in the front door.

"What's that hole doing in the garage door?" I heard her ask Barry in the living room. He mumbled something. Mum had shopping bags and brought them into the kitchen. She didn't even put them down before shouting at me. "What the hell have you been doing? That's a huge hole. It's probably broken the whole door." She said in a volume just below, shouting even though I was 5 feet away.

"It has. We had a look to see if it was still working. It's not. I'll be able to fix it, though, probably." I said, hoping to ease her volume.

"Probably? You could look more like you cared." She wasn't going to get that out of me. She looked at Rae, who was standing next to me, a partner in crime covered in red rust dust and filth. "What have you two been doing?"

"Just moving something from the junk yard. It was a bit harder to get to the garden. It was an accident. I'm really sorry, Jules. Jesus. Really sorry." Rae's apology was a bit better than mine.

"Get out of my sight. Your dad will sort this with you." We did as told. Rae went upstairs, and I went into the dining room to rest.

About an hour after mum, Del came home but not in his normal mood. Usually, he came in and changed into a tracksuit before having dinner, ready to start drinking some beers and watching sport. This time he came in flustered and clearly upset. I was grabbing a packet of Hula Hoops from the kitchen cupboard, so I saw him come straight in and sit at the kitchen table, holding his head in his hands. He looked stressed. Mum came in straight away was asking him if he'd noticed the hole in the garage. I went back into the dining room to temporarily avoid any telling off. I could hear that Del was unresponsive at first.

"David? Are you listening? Your son had destroyed the garage door. David?"

He snapped out of whatever trance he was in. "Julie! Shut up. I need to talk to you." I stayed by the door listening in.

21

"What is it?" Mums tone hadn't dropped from anger.

"There's a man on his way over here. He's going to be accusing me of sleeping with his wife." Del said, speaking quickly and quietly.

"Are you fucking joking?" Mum shouted back.

"No. I just got a call before I came in from his wife."

"Who is she? Did you fuck this woman?" My mum was getting louder but trying to shout in a hushed tone. I knew that Del cheated on my mum once before a few years ago, but it was probably more than that. I always wondered why she took him back.

"Yes." Del admitted.

"You utter bastard, David." Mum started to raise her voice even louder now.

"She's saying she's pregnant."

"Pregnant? Fucking pregnant?" Mum started slapping him. I came out to see the fight. Dad gabbed mums hands to stop her from hitting him.

"Calm down. Her husband knows and is coming round to fucking kill me!"

"I hope he does!" Mum was fighting to break free. Dad pushed her to one side, and she hit the cabinets behind her. She slipped and fell on her arse. Barry came in from the living room, and Rae was stood at the bottom of the stair case watching. Mum was crying on the floor and I was stood watching, wondering what to do.

"If he's coming here to get you, shouldn't you leave?" I said.

"Where, Paddy? Where the fuck should I go?" Del spun to me, eyes glaring.

"Get out. Get out!" Mum screamed at him. I gave her a hand as she got back up, shouting.

"Fine!" Del stood there for a second, thinking. 'Fine.'

He pushed past us all and he walked out to the front door. As he opened it, a dark BMW sped into the street and braked outside our house. Del closed the door and turned the bolt, double locking it. He looked scared.

Rae, me and Barry went to see out the window in the living room. A large bloke in his late thirties / early forties got out of the car. He was younger and bigger than Del but looked similar by the way they dressed in track suit bottoms and a t-shirt, only this guy's shirt fitted better over his huge shoulders. He went into his boot and moved things around before pulling out a metal rod, the type to work the car jack by the look of it. He strode over our front lawn and came to the window where we were watching.

He looked right at me and shouted, "Tell that fucking prick to come out here!" Barry went over to Del, who was now in the kitchen, pacing. Mum came out to look at the guy shouting at the house. This guys fury was intense. "David! Get the fuck out here!"

"You know this man?" Mum shouted at dad. "David." She walked back into the kitchen, where Del was standing, holding his face. "Who is he?"

"I sold him a policy. He's a customer."

"And you fucked his wife? When?" Mum wasn't at all concerned about this bloke outside wanting to kill dad with a blunt metal pole; she just wanted to know about the woman.

Rae and me went over to the kitchen door to watch them argue. Del looked at mum, and I could see he was scared. Not sure if he was more concerned about the guy outside who was still screaming for him to come out or if he was scared of mum finding something to hit him with.

"I've been seeing her since we met." He confessed.

"When! When did you meet?" She shrieked.

"December." Del just looked at mum. She lost it completely and grabbed the nearest thing to her, a thick glass bowl with keys and change in that was on the kitchen counter. She threw it at him, narrowly missing his head, sending broken glass and change all over the place as it smashed into the wall behind him.

Dad's valued customer had gotten around the house, and into the back garden; I must have forgotten to lock the gate after bringing the canister in. He saw us all in the kitchen standing looking shocked at mum. I picked up the phone and called the police. When I was on the phone, the man started smashing the kitchen windows with the pole. Rae screamed and ran to hold onto Barry, who held her tightly.

"You fuck my wife you fucking scum bag?" the guy shouted through the hole he made in the double glazing.

"The police are on their way!" I shouted.

"Fuck off, Mark. The police are coming!" Del shouted.

"I don't give a fuck about the police!" He shouted.

He walked further round to the side door and kicked it. It swung open, splitting the wood and cracking the glass, making a huge crash.

This guy, Mark, had cut himself with glass, so already had blood on him. Del stood by the kitchen table as Mark came at him. My mum was stood in the way and started screaming at him to get out, a strange turn of allegiance... I went to grab mum and pull her away from the action. Mark must have thought I was coming to stop him because he clouted me with the back of his left hand, sending me into one of the counters, splitting my head open. Blood ran down into my eye. Mum screamed and went at him, but he just pushed her down too. I wasn't really aware of time anymore. Del made a move at Mark with a right hook, and they got into a brawl.

They were shouting as they fought. They ended up on the ground and were punching each other in the chest and stomachs. I wriggled away towards the hallway and pulled mum with me. Barry helped me up, and I pulled mum with me. Mark was on top of Dad raining punches down onto his arms, and a couple got through to his face. Dad got a punch to Mark's ribs, and he yelped like a dog. Then dad lifted his knee, sending Mark forward into the broken glass behind him. Dad got free and crawled to the other end of the kitchen.

Police sirens were on the scene pretty quickly, and Barry let them in through the front door. Mark was covered in broken glass and was almost completely red, covered in his own blood by the looks of it because dad only had blood coming from the side of his mouth. The police piled into Mark and pulled him out of the house.

22

A policewoman came and saw to mum and me. Del was getting up from the floor, dusting himself off when little cuts on his arms from the glass started to bleed. He had taken some big hits to the face, so his nose started to trickle blood while he stood getting composed. A policeman came back in, walked him over to the kitchen sink, and grabbed a wet tea towel for Del's nose. He looked over to the kitchen door and scowled.

"Thanks a fucking lot!" He shouted at Barry. The policeman then handcuffed Del and dragged him out of the house. "This is my fucking house. You can't arrest me for fucking protecting myself!"

"Get out and stay out!" My mum shouted.

An ambulance came and wanted me to go to the hospital, but I didn't need to or want to, so I stayed after getting checked for concussion by the paramedic. The police and paramedics were working frantically, all wearing masks and gloves. Everything was manic.

The police were in there taking notes for about an hour. We all had to speak to an officer. My chat lasted for about 10 minutes with my mum next to me. I could see another policeman speaking to Barry, who was awkwardly giving his side of things.

Mum had a look of disoriented fury. The maddened look in her eyes occasionally switched to one of hurt. One minute she'd focus to see if I was okay, then be off somewhere else a moment later.

I went out to the front to see Del get driven off when a white Mercedes pulled up to the house. A woman was in the car and without stopping she went down the end and turned around. I thought that was probably the woman who was married to Mark. She saw the police and just got out of here. The police didn't notice.

After a while of us sitting around, the police came

into the living room from taking pictures in the kitchen and asked mum and Barry to come in tomorrow morning and make a formal statement. They needed us to bring all of our ID's. I looked at Rea, knowing that the story of her being Lucy would be ruined as soon as the police saw her ID. Barry's face looked calm and agreeable, but I knew he must have been shitting himself inside. The last thing people like him wanted was to be around the police. The night had been crazy but also madly amazing. Del getting caught and beaten up AND Barry potentially caught all in the same evening was more than I could have dreamt for!

23

After the police left, I stayed up in my parent's room talking to mum for a bit, but she mainly spoke about Del and how he had always been like and that. She felt stupid and angry with herself. She said she stayed with him because of me but then five minutes later admitted she loved him and felt like if she tried harder, he would stay faithful. She apologised for me getting hurt but mainly ranted about him.

Rae and Barry stayed out of it.

Mum had drunk a bottle of wine while talking to me and seemed like she would fall asleep, so I left and went downstairs. All the action that day wiped me out.

Before drifting off, I was thinking about how chaotic the last week has been. I was enjoying it, weirdly. Everything was much more interesting than normal. The next day in the police station was going to be curious. I wondered how were Rae and Barry going to keep their secret any longer?

My eyes were closed, and my body was drained, ready to slide into a deep, well-earned sleep when the door crept open. I didn't need to open my eyes to know who it was because Rae's Australian twang whispered in.

"Pads?" She came in a bit further, and I leaned up.

"Hey. You ok?" I whispered.

"Yeah." She came close and knelt down next to the inflatable mattress. "We're leaving." She whispered back.

"What?"

"We're leaving. Barry wants to leave in like 2 minutes. We're taking a car."

"Are you serious?"

"Yeah. I just wanted to say bye."

"Rae, you can't go. The police need to speak to Barry about earlier, and you can't steal a fucking car on top of everything else. Do you know how much trouble you'll be in?" I was trying to whisper, but it came out louder in the urgency of the moment.

"I know. Crazy, right?" She didn't seem to care.

"Where are you going?" I asked.

"Don't know. We're just going to head north. Apparently, it'll be cheaper and easier for Barry to find work."

She had no idea what The North was like. Barry was delusional. I had no response to any of this. It was the maddest thing I'd ever heard. Tomorrow morning mum would wake up, see that Barry and his fake daughter had stolen a car and left in the middle of the night. She wasn't in a mood to be messed with after everything that happened.

Rae hugged me and then, out of nowhere, kissed me. So sad that this was my very first kiss. Then she smiled excitedly like she was off on an amazing adventure. I had questioned her sanity a few times over the past weeks but at this moment, throwing herself into this dangerous situation blew my mind.

I could hear movement outside the door, hissing voices whispering. I walked over and cracked my door.

I heard Barry whisper, "Where's the keys?"

The intensity of the situation, of the whole night, had gotten to me. I was ailing and feeling debilitated by all the pressure but needed to do something. I placed my hand over the door handle and kept it there. Something was stopping me from shouting up to mum and causing mayhem. It was that I knew Rae trusted me. The kiss she gave me was more than one of friendship. I was important to her. I sensed it. Plus, if I were a barrier for her, she'd just try and knock me down, carry on and leave with no possible chance of seeing her again. I stayed where I was and listened to them leave. Barry in a panic, and Rae casually swimming into a swirling tide.

I heard the front door open and then close, followed by the car pull out the drive and leave our street.

As soon as I couldn't hear them anymore, I got an immediate smack of awareness that everything in my life didn't matter as much anymore. The CryoShed, my mum and dad, school, none of it was as important as Rae's safety. I had been living under a roof with this guy who, knowing Rae was only 15, abandoned his family, fled the country with her and now stole a car to go somewhere else with her.

I bolted upstairs to my mum and woke her up.

"Barry's stolen the car and driven off with Rae. Her name's Rae, not Lucy. She's not his daughter."

"What? What are you talking about?" She sat up.

"Lucy is Rae, and she's not his daughter. They just pretended to get to England."

"How do you know that?"

"She told me." I felt an enormous amount of guilt admitting that.

"Who is she?" Mum was still confused by what I was saying.

"She's a girl Barry met who was miserable at home, so they ran away together here. She's 15 like me and his real daughter."

Mum became alert instantly and grabbed her phone, calling 999 and explaining what had happened, then giving the number plate and make of the car. My heart was racing. She put the phone down, and said the police were on their way over to speak to us. I told her about Rae and her life back home with a drunk mum and her dad, who just loved his guns and ignored her.

"I didn't feel like she was in danger as long as she was here. I was going to convince her that Barry was a weirdo and that she should tell her parents that she's here and go home to them."

"You can't keep these kinds of secrets. When people are in danger, you need to trust older people to make the right decisions."

She spoke with a compassionate tone. Unfortunately, that whole sentence went against all my core beliefs. Every adult I knew wasn't capable of making a sensible decision if their lives depended on it. But maybe I wasn't much better? I felt that I had been part of the problem. I didn't have a leg to stand on. My major excuse for not saying anything sooner was the worry that Rae wouldn't forgive me for grassing her up and that she would tell everyone about what I was planning with The CryoShed.

We stayed in my parent's bedroom till the police came. They had a big king size bed and huge tv at the bottom of it. It was decorated with plain colours, white, grey and black. Mostly my mums doing. You could tell the things Del bought because they were tacky. The chandelier in the middle was horrible. I remember when he brought it home as a gift to mum. She acted appreciative, always protecting his feelings.

A plain-clothed police car pulled up outside, and we went down to meet them. The kitchen was still a mess as no one cleared up after the first lot of police had gone earlier that evening, so we sat in the living room. All the questions were aimed at me. Although they didn't come with anything too hard to answer, I still struggled. I felt like I was selling Rae out. All this private information I had promised not to tell anyone I was giving away to a bloke in his 30's who looked like he spent his whole life living underground. He was in a grey suit and looked like a black and white cartoon character. He was pale with black hair and a strange note-taking technique. He held the pen at a weird angle. It was distracting. His covid mask made me imagine that he had teeth like a mole to match the aesthetic.

Mum kept me on track the whole time. First was just basic information like Rae's full name, where she was from then the details of what she told me about Barry.

"Had he touched her?"

I admitted that I saw them kiss in the car a couple of weeks ago. At the time, I only thought he was her dad, so I didn't say anything. Then came the why I didn't say anything. Just admitting that I was keeping a secret for a friend was too flimsy. I was pushed into disclosing that I liked her and didn't want her hating me. This was something the police and mum seemed to understand.

We were told that we still had to come in tomorrow and make a statement about what had happened before with Mark coming to beat up Del.

Again the police left. I had hoped I'd feel relief or a

sense that I'd done the right thing. But in fact, I felt that Rae would hate me and never speak to me again. The only slither of positivity I could summon up was while talking to the police about what Barry was like, I remembered what a total loser he was and that Rae was way too smart to let him hurt her.

24

I decided to sleep in the dining room again even though my room had been vacated. The police had a look in my room, Rae's room, before leaving. It was clear Rae had left in a hurry. She didn't have much to pack in the first place but still managed to forget a pair of trousers. The police took them and her toiletries left behind in bathroom.

In the morning, mum came in to the room to wake me up. I was already awake laying on the deflated mattress. It was nearly 10 am and we had to get down to the police station to pick up Del and make a statement. I really wasn't keen to go. I had pretty much gone over everything already. Twice. What more did they want from me?

Mum was clearly exhausted, she didn't utter a syllable all the way to the police station, and when we got there, she really only gave one-word answers. First, she went in to speak to the same police officer that came to see us yesterday after the fight in the kitchen. He was pretty normal looking compared to the one that came late last night. He was an older man in his late 50's. Clean shaved, longish grey hair and wearing a plain shirt, unbuttoned at the top, chinos and clearly couldn't be arsed with the covid regulations. He shook hands properly and didn't offer the elbow. He didn't look like a policeman, but maybe that was because he was just very chilled out. While they were talking, I sat in the waiting room. I heard some shouting coming from further in the station. Just mad shouting, no words, just incomprehensible screams. It was scary to hear someone be like that. I looked at the woman police officer walking down the hall about to go past me.

"Don't worry about that noise. He's a drunk in the cells." She said, walking past. It was eleven in the morning! Learning that dealing with crazy drunk people at 11 am was part of being a police officer was enough to strike it off of my list of career choices.

I got a message on my phone through Facebook. It was Rae.

- Hey, Pads. We've been sat in a service station for hours. Just sat in the car. I'm inside now, grabbing some food. All fine, but Barry is majorly stressed. He doesn't know where to go. Not sure what's happening. Hope you're ok. -

I replied instantly.

- Rae, mum called the police when she heard the car go last night. They're looking for it. -

Nothing straight back from her. I didn't have it in me to tell her that it was going to be a nationwide search for a kidnapper if this went on past this afternoon.

Mum came out, and I told her about the message. The police took my phone, and that was it, the friendship was blown. They thought the best idea was to try and find out exactly where she was. The police had cars heading out looking at service stations on motorways near us. The police sent messages to Rae from my phone admitting that they were the police and telling her that she needed to speak to security at the service station. She didn't reply.

The grey figurine policeman from the late-night call out came and spoke to us again. He said they would find them in a matter of hours if what Rae said was true about being in a service station car park.

I had to take a few minutes on my own in the loo before going in to do my statement. When I came out, Del was in the reception area talking to mum. I didn't go straight over, but I could see his face was a real mess. Cuts and some heavy bruising on his face had come up purple and blue. He was a big guy, but Mark was bigger. I couldn't imagine the other guy coming away with nearly as much damage. For some reason, it was Del looking angry and waving his arms while mum listened. They took the conversation outside, so I walked over to the police officer looking after us and said I was ready to make a statement.

I was ushered through the security door into the back part of the police station. I imagined it being a busy place with criminals sat on benches waiting to be charged or chucked in a cell, but there were no criminals as far as I could see. Just uniformed officers walking around and a couple of random people at desks. We took a right, and I was led into a room.

This room had bright fluorescent lights, no windows and a couple of long solid-looking sofas. Sat down on the nearest sofa was a middle-aged, woman wearing a summer dress. It couldn't be ignored that she had enormous breasts and no bra. Trying not to stare at her chest, I noticed she was drinking a massive mug of tea that I assumed was laden with sugar by the energised crazed look in her eyes.

The police officer walked me in one step, then looked at this woman and stood still.

'Thank you.' The woman said, signalling for him to leave. He took one more look at her and spun on his heels. She said nothing to me while I looked around, trying not to look directly at her because I didn't want to look like a perv. It was a struggle, her boobs were unbelievable, and I wondered if this was some kind of mad test.

On the table were colouring books, crayons, and a small box of toy cars that the police must have used for this kind of thing since 1985. I knew straight away it was a counselling session, not a place to give an official statement. I was very put out by this. No one told me I'd be getting counselling!

The woman had a vacant smile and offered me a cup of a nondescript 'juice' drink which was basically bright orange dyed sugar water. Still, I drank it just as a way to stop myself from asking to leave in a very aggressive way. I had to make sure I wasn't going to show any issues and that I was perfectly fine and normal. I'd been practising for this moment my whole life.

"I'm Nicole. I hope you don't mind if I keep the mask off for this conversation, I'll make sure to stay two meters apart." She rolled her eyes in a jokey way. I didn't respond, concentrating my hardest on keeping my eyes locked above the neckline. "Officer Stuart gave me a call and told me what's been going on at home."

She spoke with a knowingness in her voice that was instantly irritating. And who the fuck was Officer Stuart? Was that his first name or second name? I was suspicious that it was his first name, and she'd simply called him Officer Stuart to simplify it to me. In this case, she had annoyed me five times in the first 60 seconds of our meeting. This was going to go well, I thought.

"You've had an interesting couple days, Patrick. Would you like to tell me about it?" She tilted her head to a different side after every sentence like a spaniel watching a nature program, trying to compute why other animals were in such a small box. I found it extremely difficult to engage without sounding sarcastic.

I leaned back as nonchalant as I could on the hard rock sofa and closed my eyes so I could think as I spoke. "Interesting isn't the word I'd use, but you're right, I guess."

"What word would you use to describe it?" I could almost hear brain creek as the cogs turned. What a great question. You'll learn a lot from the answer. I wasn't going to fall for this.

"Unusual, I guess. It's been unusual."

"How so?"

"You know what's happened, right? A bloke came to take my dad's head off for shagging his wife and then the bloke staying at our house with a young girl masquerading as his daughter stole a car to run off together. None of that is a usual occurrence in my life. Is it in yours?" I knew after I said it that the last bit was a bit needly and might show stress. I needed to chill out. "But it's fine. I'm just trying to stay out of it." I said. She took some notes down.

"That's a lot to go through for a young man. How did you feel after the man got arrested and your dad got taken to hospital?" She tilted.

"Well, he brought it on himself, didn't he?" I said.

"Were you scared or upset?" She tilted.

"Not really. He wasn't there to hurt me. He was after dad, so I wasn't too concerned."

"You weren't concerned for your dad?" Leaning forward with a tilt this time.

"Well, I didn't want the guy to kill him. I figured that dad would get out of it somehow. The police came, and it was fine." I was already leaning back, but if I could, I would have leaned back further.

"Okay." More notes jotted down. "You were ok with your dad getting hospitalised?"

"No, not at all okay with it, but we did just find out that he had cheated on my mum, which meant I wasn't exactly pleased with him at the time."

"I see." This was a very cliche exchange. Idiot social worker who knows nothing about me taking notes, making assumptions and inevitably getting it wrong. "Would you tell me about your relationship with his friend Barry?"

"I didn't have a relationship with Barry. My dad and me didn't look for the same qualities in the friends choose."

"So you never spent any time alone with him?" She was asking if he tried to get near me, and I knew it.

"No."

"Is there anything you'd like to talk about or tell me about home life?" She was winding down, and I wanted out of there, so I shook my head and stood up. She stood up as well and went and knocked on the door. I couldn't help but think that wasn't a very in-depth chat, seeing as she said, it had been a very interesting day.

Outside, mum and dad were sat in the reception area waiting for me. Dad got up and gave me a quick and awkward hug. I didn't look at him; I was just seeing what mum was doing. Very little. I was told to speak to my parents if I heard from Rae again. They were given numbers to councillors and different police officers. They had to stay available in case something happened.

As soon as we got in the car, my mum started talking almost under her breath but loud enough to be heard clearly. "I can't believe you let a paedophile stay in our house." Del and me stayed quiet. She clearly wanted to get angry again, but as she was driving, it was safer to let her just mutter till we got home, even Del knew that. Mum began having a conversation with herself in her head. I could tell because she was agreeing with herself and being disgusted with Del as she tutted. We drove into our road and saw there was a car outside our house with a woman leaned up against the side waiting for us.

We pulled into the drive, and the woman, blond in her late 20's came towards the car. She was wearing glasses, hair tied in a ponytail and had tight trousers on. She was the same height as me when I got out of the car. Quite good looking in a geeky way. She knew my mum and dads name.

"David and Julie Waters?"

"Yes", Del replied.

"I'm from the Times News Paper." She leaned over to shake hands. "Sophie Lawrence." As she said her name, both my parents shook her hand. Another car came round the bend and pulled up.

"We don't want to talk right now." My mum said very politely.

"I just have a couple of questions." Sophie Lawrence said, walking down the drive with us.

"Not now, thank you." Mum dragged me inside and Del scurried in after us. We closed the door.

"The fucking papers?" Del said. I walked past him to grab my laptop out of the dining room. I could hear him freak out. "The Times, for fuck sake?"

"You happy now? You'll be famous for inviting a creep into your family home. That should attract all sorts of women," Mum snapped.

"Give over. I didn't know what he was up to! How many times do I have to say it?"

"Well, you're a fucking liar, so you can keep saying it while you pack a case."

I opened my laptop and looked online at the Australian newspaper I had open from before. Rae's story was on the first page. This was how the British papers must have found out.

"Mum, look here." I turned my laptop around, and she came over to read it. We weren't named, but Barry was. Mum was physically shocked. She sat down and read the piece. I finished making her cup of tea.

"Jesus Christ." She said, eyes scanning the screen.

Del shouted from the other room. I walked out of the kitchen to see what he wanted. He was just looking out the living room window. There were about three cars and a Fox news van unloading a camera. Australian TV would, of course, be the most interested. The headline in the online article MISSING GIRL FOUND IN ENGLAND ON RUN WITH KIDNAPPER couldn't sound any more sensational, even though it summed up the situation well.

I knew this would happen; that's why I didn't say anything, to begin with. I went and pulled the curtains. Del definitely loved the attention, just as mum called it. He looked at me like I was a foreign object invading his space and turned around to put the TV on. This whole thing was exciting for him. He just wanted to see if his face was on TV.

I went up to my room to look down at what was happening. So many times before, I'd seen the front of houses on the news. No activity, just the windows with twitching curtains. I'd always wondered what the point of this was? Why did the public need to see the specific house that was in question? This detail wasn't the important part. I guess it's just to highlight that this could happen anywhere, 'look at this normal looking house, like your normal house. Be careful, or you'll end up on the news.'

There was nothing in the way of police outside even though the street was blocked and we had cameras on the front lawn. No English news people apart from the woman from The Times. She was sat in her car typing away. I could hear Mum and Del arguing again downstairs.

I laid in my bed and could faintly smell Rae on the pillow. She never wore perfume or anything, so I assumed the smell must be her shampoo or something. I drifted off thinking about how all this attention would be putting a temporary stop to my plans with The CryoShed.

I fell into a half-sleep where I distinctly remember lucid dreaming that I was at a summer camp with people much younger than me. We were all putting up tents, but I couldn't do it. All the younger kids managed it easily. My tent kept collapsing in on itself. I got woken up by mum shouting that they were ordering pizza and what did I want. I kept thinking about the dream, and even though I didn't subscribe to stuff as loose and unscientific as dream interpretation, I did feel like the tents and my life were all out of my control and falling in around me. The children an easy metaphor for my parents, I guess.

25

Barry and Rea's escape got on the ITV local news. It came after we had been alerted that they had been found. Not found in as much as Barry had handed himself in. He came to his senses after a 12 hour rush of blood. A phone call from the grey policeman lasted about 2 minutes. They said that Barry had handed himself in, Rae admitted who she was, and they were in police custody about an hour away near Portsmouth. Which was strange because Rae said they were heading north. Barry really must have lost the plot.

The report on this was made directly outside our house by a local correspondent who had set up next to the Australian Fox News team. The report was live, so we watched it, and I'm sure Del was tempted to poke his head through the curtains. It was surreal seeing our house on TV and actually quite strange watching TV with both my mum and dad. Mum was starring angrily at the TV and Del standing up walking around as he watched it. It was big news and was the only thing they spoke about apart from the latest Covid news.

I was getting messages from people at school on my phone from text, WhatsApp and Facebook messenger. People I've literally never spoken to before just being nosey. I signed off because I didn't want to indulge them. The guys from school who I knew were mainly taking the piss out of me and asking if the paedo touched me. Also, they were laughing that the one time I knew a girl she's mentally disturbed. All this was predictable and reaffirmed my complete indifference to all the friends I had. Neil called, which I ignored and then just texted asking if I had at least banged her before she left?

After the TV report, the gravity of the situation finally hit Del. I don't think he ever thought he would be named or brought up in the news, but the reporters had a lot of information that he didn't think they would have gotten. Someone in the police must have talked to the press. Del started to blame me, saying that I should have said something about Rae when I knew. This was predictable from him. Blaming me for him inviting a head case to stay in the house with his family. It was at this point my mum went upstairs and came back down with a suitcase.

"Call a cab and go stay somewhere else for a few days."

"What? I'm not leaving with all them out there!" He said.

"Yes, you are. You're leaving right now, or I'll go out and broadcast to all of them that I'm kicking you out because you knew what Barry was up to." She looked serious.

"You can't do that." Right then, mum walked to the front door and opened it. Del ran and closed the door waving to the cameras quickly. "Okay. Fine, I'll call a cab now. Give me five minutes."

I stayed around downstairs just to see if he was actually going. He called a cab, and a few minutes later, he was gone. Seeing him leave was brilliant. He got into the cab, trying his best to cover his face. I couldn't help but laugh.

Mum came up to my room with a cup of tea and a packet of biscuits. They weren't for me. She sat on the end of my bed and dipped chocolate digestives in the milky tea. She seemed to have calmed down. She turned and looked at me and said, "Are you alright, darling?" When it was just the two of us, everything was better.

"Yeah, I'm alright," I said.

"I'm sorry about all this."

"You've got nothing to be sorry for. None of this is your fault."

"Hm."

From that reaction, I deduced she blamed herself a little. Out of everyone staying under that roof she was the only one who held no responsibility for all the shit going that happened. Even I knew what was going on with Rae long before everything turned into an international news story. Mum knew something was up all along, and I didn't say anything. Now she was blaming herself for not knowing. Or blaming herself for not knowing about what was going on with Del's affair. We sat for a while not saying anything until she got up and kissed me good night.

I went downstairs and watched the news, waiting for our house to get back on. No Del, Barry or Rae in the house, my room back, the liquid nitrogen in the shed, everything was looking good for me, but after seeing my mum defeated, I felt down about everything.

I missed Rae already, and I couldn't do any work on The CryoShed in case any of the cameras caught me. I didn't want the media to find out about what I was up to. All this attention was enough for now. I started to think that when I was frozen and the press found out they'd come back and it'd be more stress for mum.

26

The next day I woke up late to the sound of my mum talking to someone on the phone. It was Del. He had been called in for more questioning at the police station. He wanted to come and get the car. The press had all left the house now. Another story to report, no doubt. He was clear to come back and get the car. I wanted to be out when he arrived. I needed metal for the soldering I was going to do to the canister me and Rae rolled down into the shed a few days ago.

I went out to the shed and took inventory of everything I had and the work that'd been done. The main thing I concentrated on was turning the canister into my hibernation chamber.

I came back inside and went up to my room, and made an update to the blueprints. I had some concerns about the whole contraption being strong enough to last 100 years. To make sure I was going to live after the freeze, I thought I had better enlist some help from professionals. So right before I go into the freeze, I'd send an email to the Cryogenics Society to see if they would check in on my CryoShed every couple of years to make sure the integrity of the build held up and that I was completely frozen. That would ease my stress. The Cryogenics Society would love my ingenuity and be more than happy to help.

The new blueprints were a little messy because I wasn't able to get some of the equipment I had originally planned for. The substitutions and allowances I had made meant that some of the kit wasn't what the scientists would probably use. My revised plan was to get the temperature inside the shed to drop rapidly and freeze me to my core then for an Evaporative Air Cooler to keep it at that temperature for the rest of the time. I couldn't have a perpetual amount of liquid nitrogen being pumped into the shed. So I drew up new blueprints with this plan.

The rest of the morning, I made the inside of the chamber that I'd lay in clean and comfortable. Then I started to chip away at the rust and dirtiness on the outside of the canister. At the moment, it still had a gaping hole on the bottom end where my feet would be. I needed to plug and solder that. The hole that was going to have the freezing air fill the canister would be just over my head and another at the bottom. I had devised a tube system that would connect to the open flasks of liquid nitrogen so as the liquid nitrogen boiled, the -100c gas would travel into the closed chamber, keeping the inside completely frozen and fast. This is what is freezing me. The air cooling unit I would connect to the power would keep the room below freezing.

My comfort wasn't a huge concern because I would take sleeping pills to make sure I'd sleep as soon as the whole process was in motion, but I didn't want to wake up with back pain in 100 years either.

The inside of what was the shed needed a clean up too. I had walked into the shed from the garden with trainers on, so the floor was filthy. It needed to be completely spotless in here.

One issue I had that I could work on while I waited for the rest of the equipment to arrive was the door. It needed to be airtight so only a minuscule amount of the cold would escape over time. At the moment, the hinges meant it was giving away a substantial amount of cold air. When I walked into the shed, I could close the door and solder it closed from the inside, but then it'd be loose on the other side. This was going to be an issue that needed thinking about.

I had other concerns like the warmth from the sun during the summer. The current exterior wasn't the best to combat this. The surface on the outside needed to be reflective of sunlight like the arctic snow. The whole of the shed needed to be covered in permanent white paint. Reflecting not absorbing sunlight was the key.

With the mornings work done and inventory taken, I went inside to eat before heading out to the hardware shop. Mum was in her dressing gown and making a cup of tea. I could have sworn she was dressed earlier. Obviously, she had decided there was no point as she just wanted to stay in bed anyway. She gave me money to pick up some other bits from the shops as I was going out. I knew I'd have to take a cab back with everything I was bringing home.

Halfway down the road to Ranjeet's shop, a car went past me, and I saw Del in the back seat on his phone. He saw me but kept going. I felt a strange satisfaction from his cold shoulder. He must have still blamed me for everything. I did laugh to myself that in his deranged brain, I had something to do with the problems in his life right now. It would have been great if I was the engineer of his downfall. I'd revel in that, but he had stitched things up himself.

Even when laughing to myself about Del being in the shit, I still managed to fit in thoughts of Rae every five minutes or so. I had never spent that much time with a girl before. I wanted to be with one, physically. I thought about that constantly before meeting Rae but spending time with her gave me a small insight into why men want to spend so much time chasing and being with women. She was so mysterious. Even after I knew about her life, her loneliness at home and detachment from her family, I still felt like I knew nothing about her. What she was doing and thinking behind closed doors was what I ended up thinking about most of all. No matter what came up when I searched on google about women and how to attract them, all the advice became useless and meaningless whenever I was around her. I had an urge to be close to her, to make her laugh and ask questions. The advice about being disinterested and aloof was impossible to adhere to. How could I act disinterested when all that I thought about was seeing past her deep dark eyes and into her brain? Especially now! What was she thinking right now sitting in a room with social workers like the one who met me?

The news said that her family was informed that she was safe. She told me they knew she was safe anyway, but being in police custody is safer still. I wondered if the police were as perplexed as I was as to why she was over here in the first place, leaving her home with Barry... BARRY.

Out of everything that had gone on, it was still ridiculous to me that she liked Barry. He was such a loser. Not handsome enough for Rae. I doubt asking Rae what she saw in Barry would have been high up on the polices list, though. They'll want to know if he touched her. A couple of nights ago, when they left in the car, I thought that he would use this as a last chance to do something to her. Maybe they decided to do it as they knew they'd be caught. I didn't know. She was unpredictable. I was a little bit surprised that she had even turned herself in when Barry did. She had it in her to leg it and find her own way. He probably begged her not to because it wouldn't be a good look if he turned up without her; the police would have turned it into a murder inquiry. No doubt she would have been fine if she had to go on the run.

Ranjeet was at the front counter as usual. He was a really lovely man but reading the paper was always more important than helping customers, so he didn't even notice me walk in. I knew where everything was by now, anyway. Everything I needed was there for a change. Painless visits to this shop didn't exist, so I should have seen what was coming when I went up to pay.

"Isn't this your family name? Waters. Is this your family?" Ranjeet had the local paper out in front of him with a picture of my house and a mugshot of Barry next to it.

"Yeah. That's us." I said, holding my money out.

"You let this man in your house? Was that the girl who was here with you?" Ranjeet said energetically.

"Well, I didn't know what was going on. None of us did. He lied to us." I felt like I had to explain even though I didn't have to. I had an immediate compulsion to defend my family.

"He lied? I see. These people are liars. They prey on the weak and lie." Ranjeet seemed quite affected by what had happened. "To come into this community and behave like this.' He slammed the paper down. 'is disgusting."

"Yeah. We were pretty shocked." Talking about it was making me sad and angry, especially with Ranjeet. I liked him, but I didn't want to talk about my personal business with him.

"Shocked? I would say so. What are you going to do now? Will your parents stay at the house?" These questions were getting well out of hand.

"Why wouldn't they stay at the house? What's the house got to do with what happened?" I was getting a bit annoyed by his questions; they made no sense to me. I just asked to pay and got out of there.

On my way to the local Co-Op I was getting more angry thinking about Barry. Not only had he brought a load of unwanted attention on my family and me, but back in Australia, his wife and daughter must be getting all sorts of aggravation from this.

I started thinking about an alternate reality where Barry did bring over his 15-year-old daughter, and I got on well with her, and we had a summer fling. We would have practised a load of techniques for when I met a girl from England who wants to have sex or even just be fingered by me. It would be great to have done everything with a girl who can't tell people I know how terrible I was. But that didn't happen. Instead, Rae was here with all her messed-up-ness. I stood no chance with Rae. So many factors were against me right from the off. But the real daughter of Barry probably would have warmed to me and eventually fancied me. I've never had time to really work on getting a girl to like me. Even though not many boys liked me, I made a conscious decision not to make lots of friends with idiots. It's different when I want people to like me. Then making friends is actually easy. Acting stupid, asking questions that you know people want to be asked, then listening to them drone on. That's how you make friends.

My thinking in the cab on the way back home turned to leaving mum alone to deal with the fall out of this. Now she'd kicked Del out, she was going to be alone. If no one were there with her, she'd get lonely and could slip into depression. I didn't want that. On the other side of the coin, she might not have been able to meet someone new if she had a son at home cramping her style. It would be a little while before Del's footprint would be gone from the house. A lengthy divorce, probably.

These minor doubts disintegrated once I remembered that if I stayed and waited any longer, I'd have to face the music at school. I was supposed to be at a summer school this whole summer. I had intercepted a letter saying my parents should schedule a meeting with the headteacher about how I should progress in the next year, dropping back a year. No way was I doing that!

I got back to the house. Both our cars were parked outside, Mum's car, the one Barry stole was returned and another one I didn't recognise. I went around the back and took my bag down to the shed before going back to the house and in through the back door with mums shopping.

Mum and Dad were in the living room talking to some people. Everything going on was painfully intriguing, so I slowly approached the living room to see who it was. They were sat with a man and woman facing them on a couple of chairs brought in from the kitchen. The man was heavy set in a thick beard and glasses. He looked uncomfortable in his mask and gleamed in sweat even though he had his sleeves rolled up. The woman was young but looked very serious. Tight ponytail, and I could tell she was short even when she was sat down. When I got in, Del stood up to welcome me with a hug. I didn't move, so he leaned over uncomfortably far to reach me and put his arms around me.

"How're you doing, son?" He said loudly.

"Fine." I looked at mum, not knowing what was going on. I figured he was doing this for the benefit of whoever this man and woman were.

"This is Phil and Mary from Social services. They are telling us what's happening with Rae now." Mum said to me.

Phil waved and took off his mask briefly to show

he was smiling at me. Mary's greeting was to passive-aggressively cross her legs the other way. Mum patted the spot on the sofa next to her, so I sat in-between her and Del.

"Yes, we've been with Rae since she came in," Phil said to me. I nodded.

"Where are you keeping her?" I asked.

"A hotel near the police station in Portsmouth, but we're actually going to be moving her to a hotel near to the airport where she'll stay with her mum when she arrives tomorrow," Phil replied.

"She's doing fine." Mary leaned into me as she spoke, squinting as though she was pressing her words on me, so I fully grasped them.

"That's good." I knew she would be extremely upset that her mum was coming over to be with her. I looked at my mum, not really knowing what else to say. I couldn't tell if my parents were in trouble. We sat in silence for what felt like a long time. Mary then moved in closer to me, sitting right on the edge of her seat.

"Rae said you and her were friends..."

"Okay." I wasn't sure if this was a question or an accusation.

Phil came in with a completely different tone. "Yes. We've spoken to her a lot, and we think it would be good for her to have a friend to talk to. She's only got police and us to speak with at the moment."

These two were playing some strange version of good cop bad cop, but this situation didn't call for it at all. "Would you like to come and see Rae for a couple of hours?"

"Yeah, sure." I was behaving very low key. Del was very happy that I was going over for some reason. He was probably just relieved that these two weren't here to determine if he was a perve as well as his mate.

"Is that alright, Mum?" Phil asked, addressing my mum as MUM, which was so unbelievably weird and creepy. I looked at mum, and I could tell that she was equally grossed out by it. But she said it was fine, so I was allowed to go with them to the hotel and see Rae.

They wanted mum to come with them, but she wanted the house to herself. She made Del leave at the same time as us.

27

Mary drove us down to Portsmouth like a total nut case. She was up the back of any cars in front the whole way there. I felt I had to cling on to survive. Phil always turned fully round when trying to talk to me, and seeing as I was sat directly behind him, he looked uncomfortable for the whole journey. I didn't trust someone that nice.

An hour of listening to Phil ask me questions about what I liked - football? No. Pokémon? No. Grime music? No. He wasn't used to dealing with someone whose interests were as unusual as mine. I might have talked a bit more if it wasn't for that. I had started to feel nervous about seeing Rae again.

Last time I saw her, she kissed me. It might have been just before she ran away with another man, but she still kissed me, and I was sure that counted for something. While Phil asked me inane questions about what I've been doing over the summer, I thought about what Rae and I talk about.

The hotel she was staying in was a big Ibis just off the motorway. There was a couple of police cars sat out front, and we parked in a spot saved for us. There were no other cars parked. We walked straight in past the reception and to the lift going up to the 1st floor. It seemed like there was only one member of staff and no other guests.

We got out of the lift, and there were two police standing outside a hotel room, one man and one woman. The policeman was obese, so much so that the stab-proof vest he had on had more fat pouring out the sides than it covered up. The woman was normal and very smiley.

"Hi Sam, Sam." Phil chuckled as he spoke. He turned to look at me and said, 'They're both called Sam.' He laughed again and waved at them. Ordinarily, I might have found this mildly funny, but the fact he got amused by it made it annoying and tragically unfunny to me.

"Phil." Big fat Sam nodded while acting very serious.

"Hi, Phil. Hi, Mary. You coming in?" The woman police officer said like she was the only normal person here, although I stood there thinking that she meant going in, not coming in, the idiot.

"Yes please," Phil said all jokily. She rattled a knock quickly then unlocked the door. Phil let me in first.

The room was in complete disarray, a total mess. On the floor were plastic bags, clothes with labels still in, food, wrappers, all kinds of trash scattered about. Rae was on the bed watching the TV. She looked up from the screen, saw me and excitedly jumped out of bed and hugged me.

"Paddy! How are ya mate?" She said, holding on to me.

I didn't say anything; I just hugged her back. Clearly, she didn't blame me for the situation. "I thought it was those idiots outside again when you knocked." She was speaking so her chin was rubbing against my neck. I could feel that I was getting a hard-on straight away. I pushed her off me and smiled.

"Come in, sit down."

Phil and Mary followed in and stood looking at us. I sat on the end of the bed. Rae up at the other end. There were newspapers from the past couple of days out open on the bed, open on the pages that spoke about Barry and her. She saw me looking at the papers.

"Crazy, isn't it? They couldn't be getting the whole thing any more wrong. I told them he never touched me and that I loved him, and he loved me."

I looked at her and the half-eaten delivery food that hadn't been taken away. She was high from the situation and the sugar from all the snacks she'd been eating. I doubted that she had had an avocado in days.

"Yeah, we had people at the house with cameras. Australian and English channels."

"Aw fuck. I'm so sorry." Rae looked over at Phil and Mary and smiled innocently. "Can't we talk on our own?"

"I don't think so, Rae. We need to keep your visits

supervised." Mary said apologetically.

"But why it's just Patrick?" Rae smiled and grabbed my shoulder, shaking me like she was proving I was the Patrick she was talking about.

"I know, but we should stay anyway." Mary said a little more firmer.

"What do you thinks going to happen? I just want to talk in private with my friend; otherwise, what's the point in having him here?" I felt like that was a good enough point, and Phil had actually already started to back up towards the door. "What do you thinks going to happen? He's like my brother, for Christ sake." Not what I wanted to hear, but it did the trick. Mary took a look at me and figured Rae was right.

"Okay, but we'll be back up in an hour," Mary said, buying Rae's innocents. They both turned and walked out.

Rae walked over to a plate on the floor and picked up a half-eaten burger. "So tell me what happened when we left? They told me your mum heard us leave?"

I put on my innocent face and raised my eyebrows. "Yeah. She came downstairs when you drove off and then came into my room. I acted asleep and said I didn't hear anything. But she went outside and saw the car was gone."

"Ah shit. That quickly? The police must have been onto us from the start." She sat back down, eating massive bites out of the cold burger. "Do you want anything? I get as much food delivered as I want."

"I'm ok. Maybe in a bit." I was actually starving but still uptight thinking about lying to Rae.

"Barry was paranoid as soon as we were in the car together." She was so nonchalant about everything.

"Why did you leave, and why did you steal the car? You would just be in more trouble?" I asked questions that I kind of already knew the answers to.

"He didn't want to go to the police station with me, and them find out I'm not his daughter, so he thought we could just run away and hide for a couple of months till my birthday and then I was legally allowed to stay."

"But the police would be after him all the time, so he wouldn't have been able to get a job or anything."

"Yeah, that's what he realised the next day before turning himself in." She had finished her burger and put the plate back on the floor. She leaned back and breathed out heavily. "He had gotten quite weird during that day anyway."

He was weird anyway, but I felt some hope in all this now she had noticed, so I asked, "Like how?"

"I don't want to say. It was just really uncomfortable. He was stressed and being different with me."

"Did he hurt you?" I asked keenly.

"No, not hurt, but he was just heavy with me when he's always been... soft with me, I guess." She had a look on her face suggesting this heaviness wasn't welcome.

I wanted to know exactly what she was talking about. It was horrible to think of her in the car alone with him touching her, which I'm guessing is what happened. I didn't say anything while I waited for her to carry on.

"But after he calmed down, we just drove to a police station. I wanted to go back to your house, but he wouldn't."

"I think he made the right choice in the end." Rae looked at me confused, so I changed subjects. "Mum's been mad for days after that thing with dad."

"Oh, yeah. Completely forgot about your dad cheating on your mum! Crazy." She was bouncing again. Her emotions were all over the place. The situation she had gotten herself in was partly exciting to her and partly a nightmare. She was swinging between the two states of mind right in front of me. "So what's happening at your place? With your dad? What about your cryogenics shed?"

"Well, dad's been kicked out. He's in a hotel as well. And I'm back on track to finish everything up in the next week. I've just got to put everything together and do a test run, and then I'm ready. Should be ready in a couple of weeks."

"Jesus. So you're going to be in the deep freeze in just two weeks?" Rae said, leaning forward.

"Yup." When she said it, I felt a rush of nerves, fear and excitement. Rae looked at me like she wanted me to talk about it more, and this sudden rush energised me. "The thing about it is that I'll go unconscious and just wake up in the future like having a normal nights sleep. That's the bit that's most exciting. I'll still be me in every way, just technically 100 years older."

"Wow. That's crazy." She leaned back on her bed. "It really takes guts to do something like that. I wish I could go with you. I'm going to be under house arrest for the foreseeable future, no doubt."

"Have they said you're staying here or going back to Aus?" I asked.

"They've not said for sure, but the feeling is that they won't need me here to do the trial for Barry. I can testify via a link because of my age. I want to stay here, though. I'll move to London one day for sure." I nodded with her. "I was thinking," she held back, looking down and holding onto a pillow briefly.

"What?" I asked, looking out the window at the car park.

"Are you a virgin?"

"That's completely out of the blue." I looked at her, and then I adjusted my position and looked away as casually as I could. "Yes. Yeah. I am a virgin."

"I thought so." She said, nodding her head.

"Well, you know I don't know many girls." I defended myself.

"Yeah, exactly. I know. Sorry. I didn't mean it how it came out." The vibe in the room had gone a bit edgy. I wasn't sure what was going on. She seemed nervous. Not like how she usually is. "Me too."

"You are as well?" I asked, and she gave a small nod as she looked down at her hands resting in her lap. "Yeah, I thought so because of what you said the other day about Barry and you."

"I could have done it with guys back home but didn't want to. They are all horrendously gross." She screwed up her face but then looked at me and smiled. "Will you find me in 100 years when you come out of the freeze?"

"I don't know. I'll try. With medical advances, you'll probably still be alive if you stay healthy, so yeah, I guess I'll be able to find you."

"So I was thinking that if you promise to come and find me when you're out of the freeze, then we should have sex now and then again in 100 years." She was laughing, so I assumed she was joking, so I laughed as well.

"Yeah, I'd do that." I laughed.

"Okay. Let's do it." She said seriously.

"What? Have sex?" She nodded. I exhaled apprehensively, "When?"

"Now. In here." The instant she said now, an erection flashed into my pants.

"Yeah, ok." I stuttered out my words.

Before I knew it, I was standing by her bed. She moved over to me, and we started kissing with her kneeling on the edge of the bed. She pulled me down, and I sat on the side of the bed with her. I had no idea what to do with my hands. She was leaning on hers. I was half turned around and needed to manoeuvre, so I could face her. My mind went from thinking about what was going on to trying to remember every article I'd read online about how to please a woman in bed, how to kiss and where the erogenous zones are. All these gold nuggets of information I was sure that I stored away in my brain completely vanished as she put her hand on my back as she kissed me. I swung myself around and kneeled on the bed, putting my hands around her waist.

She leaned back, and we kissed for a few minutes until she said, "We should be naked?"

"Yes," I confirmed.

I went to take her t-shirt off but she pushed me backwards and took her own top off. I was still wearing a jacket, so that came off, and so did my t-shirt.

I moved over to Rae again, hoping that the push-ups I did over the summer had made me look less of a boy and more manly. Rae took her bra off, and we kissed again. She pulled me closer to her, and our chests touched. I started taking in the details of her body. Her skin on mine felt amazing, and she seemed to know what else to do all the time. I knew that a man should take control, but it was impossible. Rae was going through the checklist quickly. She undid my jeans and then hers. We were naked, and then I thought that I didn't have a condom and that there was no way she had one in this room. I thought that if I brought it up, she would stop. I couldn't risk that. She held my boner in her hand and moved me right on top of her, then pulled me to just about to go inside her.

I felt so nervous about cumming straight away because my dick felt like it would explode in her hand. I was shaking and sweating so much; she wasn't at all. I just kept asking if "That's nice?" and she just said "Uh-huh" every time. Then she moved her hips, pulling me into her. Then suddenly, I was having sex, pumping her with my hips. She stopped me for a few seconds and grimaced a bit, but then she said to keep going. I couldn't breathe, and then I knew it was coming, but it happened fast. I had no control over it. I came, shaking, losing the strength in my arms and fell with all my weight on top of her. I couldn't see for a second, and I felt like crying. I didn't though; I just apologized while my face was in the pillow behind her head. She kissed me and laughed.

This was so different to doing it on your own. This was a full-body experience affecting every sense. I couldn't focus on anything at that moment, just the amazing, dense pleasure in my groin.

After a few seconds she pushed me up. I leaned up, and she looked down at my penis coming out of her. It was a bit of a mess. There seemed to be some blood down there. Suddenly she shouted, 'Oh shit!' then jerked up, smashing her forehead into my face before sprinting into the bathroom. Her head hit my nose right on the bridge. Within a few seconds, my nose was bleeding. A few drops fell on the sheets where I was sat. I wiped my nose on the pillow, but it kept bleeding.

"Sorry! I'm ok." She called out from the bathroom.

"Are you ok?" The voice of Sam, the woman police

officer, called through the door. Then I heard the plastic key go into the key reader. She was coming in. I was naked and the bed had blood spattered around on it as well lots of my semen! I jumped up to put my clothes on, but I was never going to be quick enough. "What are you... Oh dear."

I was putting one leg into my jeans and fell over trying to put the other one on. There was blood on my hands where I'd been holding my nose; it dripped down onto my chest and around my mouth as I fell onto the floor. The other Sam then came in and saw me on the floor with my arse on a broken plate and one leg in my jeans, covered in blood. The policewoman knocked on the bathroom door. "Rae, are you ok?"

"Oh my god! What are you doing?" Rae screamed out. "I'm fine. Go away!"

I was fumbling around for my t-shirt and managed to stick that on while they were checking on Rae.

"Go away!" She screamed again.

They looked at me. "It's just a nose bleed!" I said, thinking it was important to put out that disclaimer to the Sams.

"What the hell have you two been doing? Oh my god!" She looked at the blood with her hand to her face.

I was in shambles but not naked anymore as I pulled clothes on as quickly as possible. The big fat Sam walked in the room picked up my shoes, grabbed me by the arm, and pulled me towards the door.

"They're walking me out Rae," I said as I was being pulled.

"What? No." She poked her head out of the bathroom. "Sorry, Pads. Sorry. What? You're bleeding as well?" She looked horrified and confused all at once.

"Sorry. I'm sorry," I said as I got dragged. 'Bye!'

Outside the room, I was putting on my shoes and jacket when the police called the social workers to come up and get me. I was in between thinking about the amount of trouble I'd be in and also in utter disbelief that I had just had sex! With Rae!

Phil and Mary ran up the hall towards us. Mary

went into the room, and I could hear Rae scream at her as she went in. "What are you doing? Where's Paddy? Jesus bloody Christ, mate, you are awful!" Phil then signalled to me that I had to walk with him down the hall.

"You were supposed to just be talking, like friends." He said, clearly upset.

I was as shocked by what had just occurred as he was! I said, "We were."

28

The conversation between Phil, Mary and mum wasn't something I really needed to be part of, but it was like all three of them had unconsciously, collectively decided to make my life hell for the next ten minutes. I said nothing the whole time and just took in their version of the story.

Some choice cuts from this public shaming were "We found him naked and Rae screaming in the bathroom with blood everywhere." Special mention to Mary for dramatizing that scene and leaving out any context.

"We trusted him to realise she was a vulnerable child" That one came from Phil, who took me losing my virginity as a personal stab in the back. He had a look of disappointment the whole way home. But my mum's disappointment was the cherry on top.

"He's obviously just like his Father."

Fuck you, mum was all I could think for the rest of the grilling.

I know she was in a bad mood, but it had nothing to do with me. I didn't hold it against her for long. I was dealt out a grounding until school started. She clearly didn't notice that I barely went out anyway. The only thing I was interested in doing was finishing The CryoShed. We stayed out of each other's way for the rest of the day. As far as I was concerned, I had nothing to apologise for.

Replaying the day's events that night, I thought about how great it was. All the bleeding and getting discovered by the police was actually funny. I felt fantastic. The only problem was that I had no one to tell. Rae was the person I felt closest to and not just because she was my first. She was the only person who knew about my secret plans. I felt a bond. I imagined seeing her in 100 years. I looked on the internet at what 115-year-old women tend to look like. If I were going to hold my end of the deal up, I'd have to keep my eyes closed pretty tight. But then again, in 100 years, scientists would have probably slowed the ageing process down so much that being 115 would probably look more like 60-year-olds today. A quick google showed that some women in their 60's still looked quite hot, especially with plastic surgery.

The final part I needed for The Cryoshed was something to retain the cold levels needed for me to stay frozen. I found a top of the range Air Evaporative Cooler that was perfect, so I ordered it and paid the extra for next day delivery. This was the final piece of the puzzle. When it arrived, the mission was a go!

I was up in my bedroom, and it was nearing 21:00. I was wiped out, but something in me kept me going, and I went back to revise the letter that I was leaving behind.

Do Not Disturb D2 Patrick Waters

I, Patrick Waters, have entered into a cryogenic sleep that mustn't be disturbed for 100 years. This letter will serve as a goodbye to my family.
Mum, I'm sorry to leave you. I think you tried to be a good mother, but you could have done better in all honesty. Dad is an intolerable idiot. Just staying with him and making me live with him is a serious lapse of judgement. Saying that I do love you and maybe you'll live long enough for us to meet again. I'll be the same age, but you'll be 137.
Dad, I told you I don't like being called Paddy every time you did it, but you continued. One of us had to go, and as it's your house, it'll have to be me. That's why I bought the shed. You're not getting your sauna, I'm afraid.
I'm taking anything important with me. Everything else can be binned.
I have let the Cryogenics Society know of my plan, and they should be let into the shed to keep an eye on me every couple of years. Apart

from the Cryogenics Society, this venture needs to be kept within the family. The reproductions could be harmful to the country and the world. My cryogenic freezing will attract attention from the media and cause a stir at school, so it's best no one knew about it.
Only one month before the end of the 100-year freeze is anyone allowed to reveal what's happening.

On reflection, this sounded quite harsh. Mum had just gone through some bad stuff with Del recently. It was going to be hard enough on her that I was leaving her alone. Rubbing it in that I thought she was a bad mother as well would be devastating for her to hear. Everything I wrote to Del wasn't actually harsh enough. If I bring down the hammer on him a bit more, he might improve as a human being. He was an advocate of tough love. I'd show him a bit.

The instructions I've left are a bit flimsy and need to be shored up. Most of all, I thought I should write something to Rae. A message to say that I was thinking about her and that she needed to leave what happened behind her. She needed to find a passion and devote herself to it.

Do Not Disturb D3 Patrick Waters

I, Patrick Waters, have entered into a cryogenic sleep that mustn't be disturbed for 100 years. This letter will serve as a goodbye to my family. It is vitally important that I am kept frozen. If I thaw before science can guarantee my awakening in safety, I will die. This is an exploration mission, NOT A SUICIDE ATTEMPT OR CRY FOR HELP!! Mum, I'm sorry to leave you. At the time of my freezing, life had become stressful, and I'm hoping that without the aggravation of bringing up a teenage boy alone, you will be free to pursue new and old interests, maybe meet a new nan and

have a happy life with him. I never understood what you saw in dad. I forgive you for choosing him over me on many occasions when we could have spent time together or when you could have stopped him from belittling me. I want you to know that I'm leaving with love in my heart for you, Mum.
Dad, forget me like I know you wanted to. We were different from the moment I was born. My lack of sporting ability and my inquisitive mind didn't match yours. Instead of finding common ground or showing me any love regardless of our differences, you took the piss relentlessly and made life as unpleasant as possible. In the end, I just wanted to be as far from you as I could be. No one is more responsible for my departure than you. I'll wake up in the year 2120 thankful you won't be part of my life. I don't wish an early death on you. I just don't want you in my life. I told you I don't like being called Paddy every time you did it, but you continued. One of us had go, so when I bought the shed this was the plan. You're not getting your sauna, I'm afraid. Going forward, you need to think about your actions and the words you say because, from my point of view you are insensitive and selfish. Stop trying to prove yourself and grow up.
I had one person in my life with who I confided in and shared my thoughts with. Rae Dextegen. When I'm frozen, and in my hibernation for 100 years, I want you to forget about everything that happened in the summer of 2020, apart from us meeting and forging a friendship. Find a passion and make it your life. You are my first love. We will meet again.
I leave all my earthly possession to Rae. My bank account should not be touched as I am still alive and will be using the matured funds when I wake up.
I have some instructions on what to do when I'm

discovered.
Your first instincts will be to rush me to the hospital to try and revive me, but that would actually kill me. Once in my deep freeze, I will need to be kept below freezing because any of the cells in my body that get thawed by doctors would die. The technology needed to thaw and wake me from the hibernation doesn't exist yet. At the current rate of research and discoveries in this area, it will be possible in the next 50 years.
I repeat - A strict term of 100 years in my frozen state before being woken.

This draft would not be the last.

29

I had no idea how to get back in touch with Rae or if I would be allowed to see her again. Her mum was arriving in the afternoon anyway, so I thought she might have been tied up with her. My mum had the contact number for Phil and Mary, but I highly doubted she would let me call them to arrange another visit. It would be guaranteed to be supervised the next time.

I thought that because of how quick the first time we had sex was, Rea would definitely want to have sex again. Last time was just so short. The next time would last for hours. I just needed to get that first one out the way. From the moment I became a non-virgin I felt much cooler about having sex and not as nervous. A weight had been lifted, and now any girl who came along would be treated to a much more confident man in bed.

Everything had been built now, and the cables had been underground for a week. They were settled and plugged into the air cooler I had bought online. The cables were thick and heavy-duty. I had to dig the trench in deep and hide the entry points, so no one came and stole them. On that same note, vandalism had been something that played on my mind slightly. Lots of guys would love to come and graffiti on the metal panels protecting the interior of the shed, which was fine, but when something looks in disrepair, people think it's okay to trash further. I didn't want the shed looking like it was broken or useless at any point. So my next task was to look into what was out there to stop vandals from trashing my shed. Some lacquer was to be the last outside layer, after the reflective white paint.

I couldn't go down to Ranjeets because I was grounded, so I ordered some tins of clear lacquer online. I spent the rest of the day painting the shed in the bright white outdoor paint that I bought from Ranjeets beforehand.

My whole body ached from the repetitive brush strokes, and my head hurt from all the wandering my mind did during the monotonous task. At the end of the day, I had painted every inch in a thick sticky layer of white paint. It didn't look much like a shed anymore or anything I'd ever seen, to be honest.

I fell into bed at about 8 pm. Knackered and munching some salt and vinegar crisps for dinner. Before I passed out, I looked at my Facebook to see if there had been a message from Rae. To my shock and delight, there had.

"Hi, Patrick. My mums here now. I'm allowed to use Facebook again. Going back to Australia next week after some more legal stuff I have to do with my mum. FML. Don't think we can hang out after yesterday. Hope your nose is ok. I saw the blood. Sorry."

I replied, "I'm grounded after what Mary and Phil said to my mum, so can't come to see you anyway. I'm going to be ready to freeze next week."

Rae replied, "OMG, Yeah. Crazy. We'll both be gone from here then."

I replied, "Yeah. Crazy. Wish you were here to help with the finishing touches."

Rae replied, "Me too."

That was the end of that. I wanted to write more, but I thought, what was the point?

The next few days were the longest of the summer. I painted the plastic lacquer onto the shed, making the white paint gleam with every light beam that touched it. It was kind of majestic!

Burning the blueprints down the bottom of the garden was fun. I liked making fires but didn't do it often because we had a Chris Chasey at school who made lots of fires one year, and now he was in a youth detention centre because one of those fires got out of control and burnt down the church hall. Or that was his story, at least. He probably set the thing on fire deliberately. I had thought about leaving the blueprints as part of a type of legacy, but I didn't want any copycats doing what I was doing and messing it up. I made a small fire out of dried twigs, newspaper and lit it with a lighter.

30

After two days of not talking, apart from announcing food, my mum came up to my room.

"Your dad's coming to dinner tonight."

Without thinking, I said, "You've got to be joking?"

"I'm not joking."

"Why? Why is he coming over?"

"Because I've decided it's time he came to see you."

"He doesn't want to see me. He wants to come back and stop staying in a hotel. Why are you letting him back?"

"I'm not letting him back, and if I did that's something I don't have to explain to you."

There was a pause. I was thinking of how I could stop this, but before I spoke again, she said, "And you need to sort out that bloody monstrosity in the garden. The shed!"

"What do you mean sort it out?"

"Put it back to being a shed. You've had your fun. Now make it so we can use it again." She turned to leave.

I shouted. "I bought it. I can do what I want with it."

She came back and had one foot in my room. "No, Patrick, you can't. I have to look at it, and I'm telling you to fix it, or I'll get some workmen over to do it for me."

This was a declaration of war as far as I was concerned. She wanted to tare down all I'd been working on and bring Del back. Fuck that! I had to get in the freeze soon. I couldn't live with them any longer!

It had been another couple of days without contact from Rae. I'd sent her a couple of messages. I spotted a news story about there being a Black Lives Matter protest right by where we were in Camden. I sent her a link to a video. I could see that it was delivered but not read. I asked her how it was with her mum and if she was able to leave the hotel. Delivered but not read.

The stories that were in the papers weren't negative about her, although she would've thought that being referred to as a confused young girl was negative. But they weren't so kind to Barry. His wife, back in Australia, did an interview on a national breakfast TV show. She went right through the emotions during the interview. She looked nice at first. A really good looking normal woman in her 40's, blond hair and thin. She thought he was on a work trip. They talked most days, and she didn't think too much about it. He said he'd be a month as he would spend a week revisiting family and friends. She even thought about coming over and surprising him, but he claimed to be moving around a lot. The interviewer asked if he gave hotel details, but she said they always used mobile phones so she never needed to know where he was staying. She had no idea he was staying at a friends. She said that made sense because she would have noticed if he was paying for hotels from their shared account or renting somewhere. His apparent lack of planning meant she would have found out around the time that she eventually did anyway. She got angry at his stupidity for getting involved with a young girl. When the interviewer said that he claimed Rae was his daughter to the friends he was staying with. She broke and just started crying and spluttering the words "sick, it's just sick." I was completely absorbed by it. I watched it five times on YouTube.

I was still shocked that she didn't suspect anything about Barry while he was over there. He was obviously a skilled liar. Had Rae seen that interview, I'm sure her feelings for Barry would be nullified. I questioned if she had feelings in the first place. She always said that he was harmless and a good person. He provided a way out for her, so she dismissed all the negativity. Now that he's not her way out, maybe she's already practically forgotten about him. If she were in love with him, she wouldn't have wanted to have sex with me, so I was sure she was over Barry.

As the day went into the evening, I found myself getting very uptight with Del's imminent arrival and the fact my Air Evaporative Cooler hadn't arrived yet. There were no bags packed in their room for him to take with him, and my mum was cooking in the kitchen. She told me we were having dinner together and that I had to be there. Best case scenario was that she was punishing me by putting me through a meal with him, worst case was that she was actually contemplating taking him back.

I heard a car pull in the driveway, hoping it was my delivery, but it was Del. I watched him walk up to the house. He was bouncing like he had full confidence of worming his way back in. All I could do was make this dinner as sour as possible.

As soon as he rang the doorbell a delivery truck pulled in the road. This was terrible timing. I didn't want to have to be deceitful and obnoxious, but I was forced into this position.

Del was through the door, and a few seconds after, mum called up to me.

"Patrick, your dads home."

I could hear the delivery being received and signed for by Del in his ever present sarcastic tone of what is my mental son got here?

I started my mission to make this dinner uncomfortable by wearing just my pants and a vest. I never dress this way, even in my room, but I wanted a visible show of defiance that I didn't care he was home.

"Patrick!" Mum shrieked from the bottom of the stairs. I stomped down and sat at the kitchen table without saying hello.

"Pads, you alright?" Del already had a beer going. His face was much less swollen now, but dark purple patches remained on his right cheek and around his left eye socket. Mum was over the stove, keeping an eye on the pasta. "What you been up to? What's in the box?" He asked.

"Just been looking at an interview with Barry's distraught wife." I wasn't there to mess about. I went straight in with a dig. I thought this would have knocked him, but no.

"Crazy, isn't it. He had everyone fooled." Del looked at mum, shrugging his shoulders like he'd relinquished all blame. Mum didn't respond. Barry didn't fool her, she said to me she thought something was up. But she ignored us and kept pinching bits of spaghetti, seeing if they were cooked yet.

Del moved the conversation away from there onto what he was doing? His recent sales figures being through the roof. Talking about taking us away. Mum wasn't telling him not to make any plans and that their life together was over. Had she already forgotten that a week ago, there was a bloke in this kitchen pummelling him for sleeping with his wife?

During dinner, the topic of conversation was about other friends they had and how Del wanted to spend more time with friends and take mum out more. She was eating it all up. They had forgotten or chosen to ignore the fact I had a 5ft x 3ft box delivered with no explanation of what was in it. They didn't give a shit about what I was doing. I could have been buying guns or building a bomb for all they knew. They only cared about themselves. I was too filled up with fury to eat.

"You not hungry, Pads? I heard you worked up quite an appetite the other day?" Dad was grinning. Even mum smirked.

"What?" I asked, looking at him. That grinning idiot.

"Well, your mum told me you got caught doing the dirty with Rae. She sure does have a varied taste!" He laughed to himself. I stood up and picked up my bowl of pasta. I turned it over and smashed it on the table. Ragu and spaghetti exploded across the kitchen. They both jumped up out of their seats.

"What the fuck do you know about my life, you fat twat? Mum, what have you done letting him back in the house making plans with us like we're a family? He cheated on you! Not even just once. He was seeing that woman behind your back for months. She's pregnant! He doesn't care about us!" I was screaming and could feel my blood boiling to black.

"Patrick! How I treat him has nothing to do with you!" She protested.

"It has everything to do with me! I live here! I can't leave! If he's back, then I have to deal with him. He doesn't love me. He hates me!" I was looking at mum, hoping for some sense to get into her.

"Of course he loves you."

"Yes, of course I love you, Paddy" Del reacted

"You are a fucking liar." I pointed at him. "You incessantly call me fucking Paddy even though you know I hate it! You take the piss out of me at every opportunity. You insulted Rae! You don't know the first thing about what's happened with us." He looked at mum, raising his eyebrows. "There you go raising your eyebrows. I hate you! Mum, you can't let him back in!" I was standing straight up with my fists clenched down by my side.

"You don't talk to either of us like that," Mum said as she started wiping the table.

"What has the way I'm talking to you got to do with the fact you're letting him back in after everything he's done."

Del was just looking on enjoying the defence. He didn't need to say anything. He knew he'd won.

"Go upstairs, and don't come back down till you've calmed down." That was it. I knew she was always going to take him back.

My worries about leaving her alone had perished. I needed to escape as soon as possible. I had had enough of this shit.

An hour later, Del left the house and drove off.

I knew mum would eventually come in to grill me. She came straight up as soon as Del drove off. Without knocking, she opened my door.

"Whatever has been going on with you and this girl, you can't take it out on your dad." She was angry and so misguided it angered me immediately.

"It has nothing to do with Rae and me! Are you mental? It's him! He cheated, and he's a liar, and he invited Barry to stay. Every thing is his fault, and you just let him back in!"

"What goes on between your dad and me is our business and not your concern."

"You say that like you think it's true. Are you insane?"

"It might all seem like life is black and white to you, he does something bad, so I leave him, but life is more complicated than that. He's back for reasons that affect both you and me. And if you can't forgive the people you love, then there's no hope for any of us."

She was clutching at straws, thinking I would entertain forgiving Del for anything he's done.

"I've laid down new law, and we'll work together on making this family work." She looked at me, seething, not taking any of her rubbish in. "Calm down and go to sleep!"

She walked out and slammed the door behind her. I was fuming, pacing around the small area at the foot of my bed. After a while, I started to try and calm myself down. Breathing in and out deeply. The house phone rang, which was strange for 9 o'clock. I opened my door to try and hear about who it was. Unfortunately, It would've been too quick for it to be a report of Del's car flying off the road into a ditch.

It was still a bit light outside and warm. A police car pulled up to the house. My mum walked over to it, and one officer got out. I couldn't hear what they were saying even though my windows were open. She came back in and went back outside again with some cans of coke. I didn't want to speak to her, but I wanted to know what was going on.

Downstairs, mum was still clearing up pasta sauce. The spray had some impressive reach, hitting all the way over to the sink.

"What are the police doing here?" I asked.

"Your girlfriend has run away from her hotel and they think she might have come here." She said, not looking up at me. I turned away from her so she couldn't see me smiling and ran upstairs two steps at a time. I went straight onto Facebook messenger to see if she'd said anything. No message from her. How would she even get here, I thought?

The distraction of Rae was incessant. I had to put her in the back of my mind and remember everything that was happening in my life and that she was leaving to go back to Australia anyway. It took a little while to compose myself, but once I heard mum come upstairs after clearing up everything up, I knew I could get back to finishing The CryoShed.

I had all the parts now. I was ready to hook everything up. I waited till midnight and went downstairs and into the garden. It was dark by this time, and I didn't want my mum to see me, so I didn't put my torch on just in case she was awake. I unlocked the shed and took my time getting the new parts down the hill and into the shed. It was a struggle because the Air Evaporative Cooler was about as heavy as a person, so I moved it tipping it corner to corner, trying my best to be quiet.

It was hard to focus. I couldn't risk messing it up and not connecting the right parts, so I decided on a new schedule. The next day I would connect everything, put the finishing touches on the interior and exterior of the CryoShed. The day after would be a test to see how it was all working then I would need a couple of days to get my affairs in order. So by the weekend, I'd be ready to take the biggest step of my life and transport myself into the future.

I was buzzing. In a week, all this would be over!

31

Surprisingly I slept like a log! One of the best nights of sleep I've had in ages. I woke up feeling fantastic. The prospect of leaving Del and my mum to get on with their lives without me was giving me an extra boost for the day ahead.

Before getting out of bed, I planned an itinerary for the day in my head. Nothing can get in the way of my mission, even though Rae escaping police custody was in the back of my mind. Out of bed, I attacked the day better than I had for the last few weeks. Post moisturiser, I looked in the mirror, and G'd myself up with some positive words. "This is going to be a great day! You can do this! Everything's going to work, and you'll be a huge success!" In all honesty, I was always cynical about these American types of positive behaviour, but on a day like today, I needed that little bit of extra confidence to give me a boost. I knew I'd be getting my hands dirty today, so I dressed appropriately.

It was early, and mum wasn't up yet. I made a healthy breakfast, consisting of all the fruit we had; 1 banana, a hand full of strawberries, some orange juice and a carrot went in the blender for a smoothie. I had never made one before, but I nailed it first go. I drank it with my Weetabix. Washed everything up and stepped outside. The air smelt sweet and fresh. It must have been how all the flowers blended with the smell of wet grass from the morning dew. It doesn't happen the rest of the year, only when the sun has no clouds to battle with. Patches of grass were lit by the sun, and the dew resting on top reflected the blue sky. The shadows were dark, and the shed looked magnificent, nestled in the back corner of the garden. It was a beautiful object. The futuristic cryogenic labs from movies looked a million miles from my efforts, but this was the real world, not that of fantasy where there are limitless budgets and supermodel scientists. Here there was a functioning breakthrough in science brought to the world by me. I opened up the double doors and lifted the liquid nitrogen tank onto the raised part of the shed underneath the funnel connected to the tubes for the liquid and gas to travel in. I heard the back door of the house open.

"Patrick?" Mum was up and called for me. I came out of the shed and saw her standing barefoot on the garden paving. She had a cup of tea and looked down at me and then around the garden.

"Did you want breakfast?" She asked.

"Already eaten."

"It's a lovely day." She smiled down at me and turned to go back into the house.

I went back to the shed. It was hard to see in there because it was so bright. The tinfoil I covered the inside with was reflecting and light that crept inside, and when I closed the doors it was pitch black. The reflected light wasn't too bright, so I only managed a couple of hours in the morning.

Everything was connected. The power leading in from the house to the shed was hooked up; I just had to go and flick the fuse in the house on.

I saw that the police car was still outside even though it had been a whole night and most of the morning since Rae had run away. They couldn't expect her to come here still. She'd have guessed that they would look for her here.

I was in the garage by the switchboard and took over the path connection for lights and power sockets in the attic that don't get used. I thought to myself I should add that information into the goodbye letter, so they wouldn't turn everything off.

I heard a car pull up and I heard Del on his mobile. He was just finishing up his conversation with one of his dick head mates, who apparently thought it was funny when Del said, "Yeah, she only lasted a week without me".

Him taking the piss out of my mum to someone on

the phone would have angered me usually, but I thought she was asking for it a bit after her stupidity. If it was possible, it made me hate him even more, though. I was too busy to get wrapped up in that anymore. Another car pulled up outside the house just after Del, and I was hoping it was another bloke looking to beat him up. I finished the connection, flicked the switch and walked back into the house. The second car was another police car swapping with the one that'd been there all morning.

Del shouted, 'Alright fellas.' jovially at the police. His chipper attitude was grinding on me, and I hadn't even seen him yet.

When I came back into the kitchen, he was with mum and a bag of dirty clothes for her to wash. I tried to get past without interacting with them.

"You haven't got your girlfriend hidden in the shed, have you, champ?" Del asked, pointing down at the shed, laughing to himself.

"You knew her. She was here for nearly three weeks. Now she's missing, and it's funny to you. You're sick in the head." He made some noise, and I walked out. Following me was mum, and before I got to the shed, she called over to me. So I stopped in the middle of the garden and turned around to face her.

"I know you're mad at your dad, and I appreciate that, Patrick." Mum talked softly to me for the first time in days, but I knew it was on Del's behalf, so it meant nothing. "I've not forgiven him for what he's done yet, but you don't know what he's said to me in private. We've both got work to do. He's going to try harder with you as well. But you have to talk to him with respect. He has provided for us and paid for everything you're looking at. That deserves your respect." I nodded dutifully, pretending to care about the rubbish spilling out of her mouth. "Now, you don't have to apologise right away, but you will soon. We want to get this families life back on track after everything that's happened recently."

"Yes, mum. No problem." I forced out a smile, and she turned back up and went inside. I hoped that one day she'd be able to hear herself, get this family back on track? When had it ever been on track? I wasn't there for that part, obviously.

The inside of The Cryoshed was looking amazing! The air cooler was ticking over, and the thermometer was showing that the air temperature was steadily dropping. The hum of the machine was like music to my ears. Already I could feel the room getting a bit cold! I cleared out what was left of my tools from the floor and left the padlock for the inside on the floor, and closed the door. In a last-minute decision, I used the spare plug socket to attach a light so I could see while I was in the shed before shutting myself in the hibernation chamber.

I decided not to wait for the next day to run the tests. Seeing as all the parts were connected, I could be ahead of the game if I did a run thought that evening. I went for it. I had to get the whole interior and hibernation chamber to drop temperature rapidly. I opened the liquid nitrogen tank by twisting the nozzle with protective gloves to kick start the temperature dropping. I could feel it get freezing in the room immediately. The gas smoking downwards and bellowing around the canister looked so cool when I stepped out The CryoShed. I closed the door and looked adoringly at my creation. I only had the last bit of work to be done, and that was for security.

I had some spare scrap metal and used it to line the edges of the shed doors so when they shut, there were no gaps that someone could get into to prise the doors open. The door was looking thick and imposing, hench, I thought, like a bank vault or airlock on a spaceship. I had already lined the inside of the doors with plastic, so they would seal shut.

I only had a break for about 15 minutes to eat a protein-rich lunch of cold chicken and hula hoops dipped in salad cream. That was a pathetic last meal, and I should've eaten something special but then I thought that I should probably have an empty stomach going into the freeze like before an operation.

Mum and Del were out for lunch. I heard them saying that he had taken holiday time, so they were free to do what they wanted. I knew they would be out the rest of the day drinking. I didn't get an invite. They probably used the excuse that I probably wouldn't want to come, so why bother asking. They were the same as my schoolmates but without the excuse of being 15 years old.

The police were still sat outside the house.

It took another hour for me to finish the final touches of the exterior security. I felt very tired after all the work but next on my list was to get the goodbye letter finished. I wasn't that bothered about saying goodbye to either of my parents or even Rae because I think she knew how I felt. I was more worried about people messing with The Cryoshed. The letter would be there to make sure people knew what I was doing and that this wasn't just a very odd suicide.

The day had gotten to me. I passed out while re-writing the letter.

32

Orange sunlight was shining directly on my face. It was evening sun so it wasn't too hot, just a lovely warming all over my body. I was woken by chilly sweat and some dribble on my pillow rather than by the light coming in. The beams only helped me wake up quicker. Completely by accident, I had fallen asleep for 3 hours. Looking back, this was a waste of precious time.

I looked outside and saw no cars in the driveway and no police car either. I was alone. I used this time as I usually did and had a wank. It was to be a long and meaningful one as my balls would be frozen with me just like everything else soon, so I had to relish each of my last private moments. However, I got distracted by a car pulling up, so I had to finish quickly.

The car that I heard was Del's coming back with mum. They were making noise doing something random in the house for about half an hour before I heard him walk upstairs and towards my room. I cleared up everything around me and closed my laptop. Typically he didn't knock. I was standing by the window facing him as he walked in.

"What are you up to?" He said, looking at me like I was being weird.

"Nothing, I was just going downstairs. Do you ever think about knocking?" I walked and tried to get past him, but he stopped me.

"I don't need to knock on doors in my own house." I've heard him say that before. It was aggressive and made no sense then and now. "Wait before you go down. I wanted to talk." He pushed me to my bed and sat on the end with me. "We've not spoken properly in a while," or ever I was thinking. "Lots has been going on recently."

I chose not to interrupt and let him say what he wants to say and be done with it.

"I wanted to make sure everything was ok with you. I didn't know what was going on with Barry and the girl. As far as I was concerned, that was his daughter, and he was staying here for work. He had this hidden thing going on. I hadn't seen him in a long time or spoken to him much, to be honest. He always had a thing for younger girls, but it was never a thing or a problem before, I guess. He never went below the legal limit, I don't think." Del was drunk and rambling.

"So he wasn't a paedophile when you were mates?" I couldn't help myself.

"Look, paedophile is a strong term. She definitely looked older than 15 and, and he never even touched her, it was told."

"He just kidnapped her instead?"

"He didn't kidnap her! She came on her own free will." Del defended Barry. No real surprise.

"I think the police are saying he kidnapped her." I pointed out.

"The police are making an example of him. But look. I have to see if you're ok." I noticed the word have there. "The social workers said I had to speak to you and see if Barry was ever inappropriate towards you." I was wondering why he had chosen to talk to me, but now it seemed as though he hadn't chosen at all. "I know he didn't. But you have to tell me he didn't."

"He didn't, but I always thought he was weird, and so did Mum," I said.

"Ok." He got up. "We're all going away for a week as a family, so pack a bag and be ready for tomorrow early."

"No problem." I stood up as well.

"Don't you want to know where we're going?" He turned and said before walking out.

"No, not really. I'm sure it'll be just fab." I said, trying not to sound too sarcastic.

I headed downstairs after the deep and meaningful with Del and went back out to the shed to check to see if the new metalwork was sturdy. It looked beautiful. The colours of the trees were reflecting off of the white paint. The sun was low and peaking through trees, making leopard spots cast shadows on the garden and shed. I looked on very pleased with myself. I walked over to give it a closer inspection and saw straight away someone had been messing with the lock on the door. I thought that Del must have gotten overly curious when he got in.

I was suddenly made to jump out of my skin by a hand reaching from behind the bushes at the bottom of the garden.

"Patrick!" a loud whisper called. After the initial scare, I knew by her Aussie twang that it was Rae.

"Rae, What the fuck are you doing?" She rustled around for a bit before talking.

"Is it clear to come out?'' She asked.

"Wait till I check." I ran back up to the house and had a look to see where Del was. He was in the lounge watching TV. No sign of Mum. She must have gone to bed early after drinking all afternoon. I ran back down. "Yeah, it's safe for now."

"Open the shed, and I'll run in there," Rae instructed.

"I can't. I have to wait till tonight for the temperature to drop." I didn't want to open the shed and let the evening sun warm up the inside and set me back hours. She had her belly against the dirt floor and tutted, flashing me an angry glare.

"I can't stay in this bloody bush, mate!"

"You want to sneak in, up to my room?" I suggested.

"Yes!" Rae said, moving slowly up out of the bush.

"Okay. Come up now, and I'll distract Dad." This wasn't thought out at all. I panicked slightly, thinking that she came back here to have sex with me again, which would be awkward because I had only had a wank 10 minutes ago. But I couldn't worry about that now. I just had to get her inside.

We crouched down, walking up the garden like marines entering enemy territory. Not sure why but it just felt like the right way to approach. We got in, and Rae hid behind the kitchen door, waiting for my signal. I walked into the living room and in front of Del blocking the TV.

"What are you doing?" Del asked, moving over on the sofa to get a better view of the TV.

"I was actually curious about where we're going this weekend."

"Just step to the left a bit." He waved me over. Some football was on the TV that I was partially blocking. I stepped over. "We're going to Crete, Greece." He smiled at me, very pleased with himself. "It's the only place on the planet we can go to right now, but you'll have your own room and can do what you want. The hotel has a pool and everything. You can just chill."

Stuck on an island with them two didn't sound like a good plan at all.

"Oh, that sounds great." I looked past Del. Rae was crawling along the floor. Being low down seemed to be the best way to attack this mission, but I thought speed might have been a key factor in its success as well. I couldn't signal anything to her. She just crawled silently behind Del. She was taking ages, so I had to keep talking. "Errm, will I get my own room?"

"Yeah, I just said that." Del snapped back at me, rolling his eyes.

"Yeah. Cool sounds great." I was stuck for questions. The early confidence I had in this situation had vanished. "Will we be taking a cab?" I was looking at Rae as she was reaching the landing.

"Yes we'll be getting a cab to the airport. What's your problem?" He saw I was looking at something behind him, and he turned round to look. Rae's foot was just lifting off the top stair as he turned around.

"Nothing. I'll start packing." I ran up the stairs skipping two steps at a time.

"Good stuff." Del exhaled, leaning back into his default position.

Upstairs, Rae was closing the curtains in my room when I walked in. She turned around and opened her arms, laughing, making jazz hands.

"I'm here!" She said. I walked over and gave her a hug.

"What are you doing here?" I asked, pulling back to look at her.

"I just couldn't stand being in that room with my mum anymore, so I just ditched them and hitched a ride here." As she was talking, I could see she was filthy with white paint on her hands. Clearly, she was the one trying to get in the shed.

"Who from?" I asked

"Just these guys who were on their way back to their parents from a surfing trip by the coast. Really nice guys." Rae said.

"Jesus. Where did they drop you?"

"I stayed with one of them last night, and then he gave me a lift this morning."

"You stayed with him?"

"Well, I didn't know where anything was or what it was called, so I just said the hardware shop near to the station. I walked back here from there. I saw the police car and waited."

"How long have you been waiting?"

"Well, I don't know because I fell asleep in the bit behind the bushes this afternoon." She was very happy with herself. "I'm so thirsty."

I went downstairs and made a jug of squash. With that, I brought up a load of food from the fridge and some crisps.

We talked about everything that had been going on. How her mum had been lecturing her ever since arriving and drinking wine like it was water. The police hadn't been telling them anything to do with Barry. No contact with him, obviously, and the social workers had been treating her like shit since I was there.

I was listening, waiting for a break in the conversation to make my move. She eventually got onto talking about when I was at the hotel with her.

"I was so embarrassed when you had to leave. I'm really sorry about that." Rae admitted.

"It's ok. I was a bit worried about you after." I shifted over a bit closer to her.

"I was fine apart from screaming at the police and

Phil and Mary for barging in." She said, smiling.

"Yeah." I shifted over a bit more.

"There was so much blood. I had no idea." I was half-listening to her as she spoke, just thinking about the move I was going to make. "There was a lot of blood right. Pad's?" She said.

"Yeah, well, you hit my nose," I said as I looked at where her hands were and if there were any signs being put out there to me. She pushed my chest as she spoke.

"Yeah, but it was everywhere." She laughed, and I laughed a little as well. "Patrick. We're not having sex again, so stop trying to get on top of me." She stopped me with a dull whack to my heart. I looked at her, very disappointed and slid away from her.

"Why not?" As pathetic as that sounded, I really couldn't think of anything else to say.

"Pads. We're friends. The other day was just a friend thing." She said, putting her hand on my knee. She had no idea that any touch from her made me desperately hard.

"Okay. I just thought you came here to have sex with me again." I said.

She leaned back and laughed. "Sorry, mate. It was great, but we'll do it again in 100 years. I just wanted to come here and help you before you do your thing. I thought I could hide here for a couple of days and help at night."

Her smile was so genuine it was hard to stay miserable. I was pretty disappointed, but I didn't want to look too upset.

"I'm going to do it tonight. I'm going to go into the freeze tonight." I said proudly. "Everything works, and it's ready."

"Wow, that's so soon. Obviously. Wow! That's amazing."

I sighed heavily. "Everything here is just unbearable. I've got to get out of this situation."

"So your dads back living here already?"

"Yeah. Mum just took him back, and we're supposed to go on holiday together tomorrow to bond as a family. I'm not going, obviously. He told me earlier, which is why I'm bringing everything forward." I laid back on the bed and looked over at her. She was just shaking her head.

"What's the plan then? Is it safe?" She asked after a while of us laying in silence.

"When it's dark, and mum and dad are asleep, I'll go and get into the chamber. I'll take sleeping pills before I go in, so I should fall asleep pretty quickly and completely freeze over after a few hours. Everything's set. I just need to finish the goodbye letter."

"Wow. All ready to go. Let's see the letter." I grabbed my laptop and pulled up the unfinished latest draft. I watched as her eyes moved over the writing. She reached the end. "Very serious, isn't it?"

"Yeah, well, it's a serious situation." I pointed out.

"I don't think you need to say much about what you think about your parents. Just that you're not happy and want to see the future, or something like that. You don't want to be remembered as bitter."

She had a point. The most recent draft did mention the hard feelings I had about everything that had happened recently and before. I nodded when she said she'd rewrite it for me.

Rae typed and rewrote the letter. It began to get dark, and I went to get more squash. Everyone had gone to bed, and the house was silent.

The new letter was much shorter and got to the point. She left it sounding like what I was doing was a positive life goal that I was now achieving.

Do Not Disturb — Patrick Waters

I, Patrick Waters, have entered into a cryogenic sleep that mustn't be disturbed for 100 years. This letter will serve as a goodbye to my family. It is vitally important that I am kept frozen. If I thaw before science can guarantee my awakening in safety, I will die. This is an exploration mission, NOT A SUICIDE ATTEMPT OR CRY FOR HELP!!

Mum, I'm sorry to leave you. I hope you don't find my leaving too stressful and know that it's because I want to see a new world where I can do good. I'll be able to share what life is like in the year 2020. Dad, we had our differences. We're very different people, and I don't hold it against you. Look after Mum better than you did before I left. Maybe I'll see you both in 100 years. Probably not. I'll always think of you.
I leave all my earthly possession to Rae. My bank account should not be touched as I am still alive and will be using the matured funds when I wake up.
I have some instructions on what to do when I'm discovered.
Your first instincts will be to rush me to the hospital to try and revive me, but that would actually kill me. The technology needed to thaw and wake me from the hibernation doesn't exist yet. At the current rate of research and discoveries in this area, it will be possible in the next 50 years.
I repeat - A strict term of 100 years in my frozen state before being woken. If you were to open up the cryogenic chamber, you would lower the temperature and prematurely thaw me. I repeat - This would kill me! There is no way to thaw me safely and bring me out of my hibernation.
Thank you, and I look forward to waking up in the year 2120 to do good and learn about the evolved culture!

Patrick Waters

I thought that did the trick. Not too much flair and to the point.

For the next couple of hours, we spoke about what the future would be like again, what Rae was going to do after today and back in Australia. She thought she would probably try and come back to London or move somewhere to learn a new language. Basically, she had no plan.

33

It was time. About 00:30. I checked to see if my parents were asleep. They were. I printed off the letter, signed it and left it outside their bedroom door. I also sent an email to them and the Cryogenics Society explaining what I was doing. I wanted their input to help my family when I was frozen and thought they might want to look at my work for their records.

Rae and me crept downstairs and outside into the garden. We were trying to be as low key as possible. It was a warm evening, but as we got closer to the shed, we could feel the cold resonating from The CryoShed. That was a good sign.

I had changed into my nicest clothes. A pair of blue chinos and a white shirt with a blue diagonal stripe down it. It's a classic look that will undoubtedly still be in fashion in a hundred years like it has been for the last seventy. I had the key to the padlock in one hand and Rae's hand in the other, gripping it tensely.

"You know it's really good you're here because it means the door can be double locked. I can lock it from the inside, making it near impossible to break in. You can do the outside, so we're doubled up."

Rae stood smiling at the sight of me in my nice clothes and looking pretty nervous. When I went upstairs to grab another lock, I ran into the bathroom and threw up. I was hugging the bowl for about 15 minutes. I was terrified. It had dawned on me that I was leaving everything I knew behind and that anything could happen while I was in there. The major thing that got me up and out of the toilet was that I didn't want Rae thinking I was a wimp. I stood up and took out the two sleeping pills in my pocket, swallowing them in the hopes that they would act fast.

Back downstairs, I walked up behind Rae. "You'll

have to hide or destroy this key when you lock it."

"Ok, mate. No problem." She had this almost crazed smile. She was excited to be part of this. I wasn't smiling. I still felt sick and was quivering.

I walked up to the front door of the shed and unlocked it. The doors swung open as if being pushed from the other side and suddenly, bright white light boomed out, followed by frozen fog billowing out of the doorway. It looked like I was walking into a NASA experiment!

I turned and looked at Rae. Not only was she smiling, but she was also waving with the hand holding the key. It felt like the right time, so I walked over to her and grabbed her hand to stop it waving, and kissed her. It was the best kiss I'd ever had. No teeth clashing, it wasn't noisy, and our tongues touched lightly without being messy. Typical that I had gotten good at kissing right before I was never going to see her again. I pulled away and said, "See you in 100 years." and smiled. When I turned around, I was very glad Rae was there to see it because I knew that was the coolest thing I'd ever done and maybe would ever do. I also hoped that I got the taste of sick completely out of my mouth before that kiss.

At the door of the shed, I looked back, and with the gases flowing all around me, I waved.

"You better still have sex with me when I'm old!" Rae called to me. I responded with a nervous laugh, nodded, then turned, walking into The CryoShed, closing the doors behind me.

I was the coldest that I had ever felt in my life. Painfully freezing. I locked the doors and heard her lock them from the other side. No way I could bottle it now. There was a thin layer of frosty ice all over the pipes, and the canister was frozen stiff and impossible to open at first. I breathed on the handle, gave it a shake and wrenched it open. I was very happy to see that it was all dry inside. The foam in the bottom was cold but didn't have the frost on it like the outside.

I had tested out the size a few times, but when I was laid down in The CryoPod about to close the lid, it felt too small. I reached over to the light switch and turned it off. The only thing helping me see was the tiny blue light coming from the Air Evaporating Cooler.

My heart was racing, and I was hoping the sleeping pills would kick in soon; I didn't want to be in pain from the freezing. Closing The CryoPod was a lot heavier from a sitting position, and the stiffness from the metal expanding was not helping. Even though it was freezing, I still managed to get hot trying to pull it over on top of me. Eventually, it creaked over and shut, suddenly crashing down and shaking the whole CryoShed. The internal lock was right next to my hand, and I closed it, making sure it was in place. I looked up. The window wasn't directly over my face, but I could just about see out of it and knew people would be able to see in and know that there was someone in here.

That was it. All the planning, the building, soldering, painting, the stress at home, the falling in love and the sex was over. I was to be a citizen in a new world of 2120.

Now here I was going over everything in my head as the sleeping pills started kicking in. I felt like I should have been thinking about all the science I'd be seeing when I woke up, but all I was wondering about was what it would be like to have sex with an old woman. I was hallucinating Rae's 115-year-old boobs hanging over my head and her laughing at me for sticking to my word. I was definitely feeling something in my brain as I lost the feeling in my hands and feet. I could see old Rae. That was the last image I had in my brain. She was laughing at me. Old lady Rae was laughing.

34

I started this story from a cold, dark place on my own, a bit scared, disenfranchised by the modern world and resentful towards my parents. Now I was in a hot, bright hospital room under constant supervision and still feeling pretty resentful.

After playing over all the events leading up to my freezing, I fell into a lucid dream state, probably caused by my high heart rate, fighting off the drowsiness caused by the sleeping pills. I could see the future and the amazing advances. I drifted off, hoping that I was in touching distance of a new life.

I remember thinking these crazy lights and noises must have been me travelling through time, and soon I'd wake up in the year 2120. The last thing I remember was Rae's old face cackling at me before a deafening crashing noise shook me up. I couldn't see what was going on because of the frosted window. The noise changed from a banging to a drilling. I was brutally cold but I was in a sleepy daze so I wasn't sure if I was still dreaming because it was so dark. After a minute, the drilling stopped, and I tried to wipe the frost off the window.

While trying to manoeuvre my arms to the window inches away from my face, I realized that I wasn't dreaming and that The CryoShed was being broken into. Different scenarios ran through my head. Even though I knew it wasn't possible to reanimate spontaneously, I was, at the time, not thinking straight. I thought that I might have been frozen for 5, 10, 20 or maybe 50 years. I had no concept of time.

A huge crash of metal shook me, and then some crushing by the door revealed light. I couldn't see much because the window only allowed me to look straight up. Beams of torch light streamed in. It turned out they were from firemen's helmets. I knew then that no one had paid a blind bit of notice to the note I left with specific instructions. The rage I felt at being ignored, yet again, warmed me up. I knew that my dream of being frozen for 100 years ad been obliterated.

Firemen prised The CryoShed open, and I unlocked my pod from the inside to help them. I didn't want to make it harder for them. It wasn't their fault my parents panicked and didn't adhere to my wishes. They pulled me out of the shed.

According to the news, I was blue and lifeless. Actually, my eyes were open because I remember seeing in slow motion the paramedics rush around and Mum crying into Del's chest while Rae shouted 'Sooorry!' at me.

In the hospital, I learned that I was in the early stages of hypothermia, but my fingers and toes hadn't quite frozen through and died, which I was relieved with. I could have lost them to gangrene. It turns out I was only in the shed for 40 minutes when I was broken out. At the time, I thought it was strange that my parents saw the note, but later I learned that Rae had completely bottled it and ran into the house shouting for help after I had been in there for a few minutes. She told them everything, and they called 999.

By the time I was feeling fine again, Rae had left the country. At first, I was furious at her for grassing me up. I was ready to tell her off and guilt her into feeling bad for me. But the reality of me having a go at Rae would have only gone one way. She would have shrugged her shoulders, apologised, and I would have forgiven her in the hope of some friend makeup sex.

The hospital I'm in now is for young people who've attempted to commit suicide. I'm under constant surveillance and have only just made it ok for my parents to visit after denying them access for a couple of weeks. Some of the patients here are in a seriously bad way. The Dr's think I have some deep issues that go beyond my explanation. It's extremely hard to keep my cool when talking to them, but I have to stay calm and keep to my story because it's true. They think I was suicidal, but it's the opposite. I was trying to extend my life, for fucks sake! Trying to explain to people who think you're crazy that you're in fact completely sane is very tricky.

I don't know how long I'll be here, but I have recently had some good news. Apparently, I can start back in school in the right year and not be held back because my failures have been blamed on my mental fragility. They are saying I exhibited a lot of unusual behaviour at school and was secluding myself from people. This was, of course, happening while I was simultaneously doing about eight peoples homework and planning The CryoShed.

Now I'm thinking of changing tactics to get out of here. That's why I said I'll see my parents. If I start to behave like a normal son, they'll let me go home, and I can start my new plans. Seeing as I'm going to have to stay in this time and area for a while, I want to put my new sexual experience to good use and work out a way to get over to Australia and see Rae again.

While I'm over there, I'll build some kind of transport to the future that won't be tampered with. I imagine that the vast, desolate expanses of the Outback is a perfect place to create a secret project, even better than my garden shed.

THE END

ACKNOWLEGMENTS

I wrote the first draft of The CryoShed in the summer of 2017, when work was slow. I wanted to use the time to try writing a long form story when all I had done before was short scripts or short stories. I only had the impetus and confidence to try writing a novel because my parents have always shown an, unreasonable about of belief in me. This book is specifically dedicated to my dad, Clive George Robinson aka Chez. It was easy to write the character of Del, Patricks dad, because he is the antithesis of my father who, unlike Del, is totally unwavering as a solid and supportive father. He's given me everything in his control to help power me in a direction no matter what random course I set for myself. All my innumerable mistakes have been met with an understanding empathy and logic that's made me feel like the mistake was a good thing, regardless of the outcome. I wish everyone could be lucky enough to have someone in their life like Chez. The one thing Chez and Del have in common though, is they are both top lads! Thank you Chez.

Further acknowledgements.

Alice Wheately, my love, thank you for being so positive and loving me when I'm struggling. Your smile gets me through everything and I'm not the same man without you. I would cryogenically freeze both of us for 100 years if I could.

Thank you to my good friend Simon Moore, who designed the front cover of this book and for always being there when I need help with a project. I truly appreciate it!

Thanks to Paige Lawson who worked extremely hard editing my manuscript which with my dyslexia must have been a nightmare, and whose feedback gave me great confidence in realising this book into the world.

Thanks to my little sister Leah Joyce Robinson, who drew the amazing blueprints for The CryoShed featured in the central pages of the book. They are perfect and exactly like I had wanted.

Thank you all to the friends and family who read the novel when it was still a work in progress, your feedback was unbelievably useful and encouraging.

SEAN E ROBINSON BIO

I was born in Epsom, Surrey, England but now reside in Bow, East London. I work in the art department for films and commercials and write in my spare time. I spent the early years of my working life the music industry, marketing and also touring with musicians around Europe which was fun but didn't pay the bills so at the same time I topped up my earning by labouring and bar tending.
Later, after a year enrolled as a mature student studying film I left early and I started to write short scripts, direct music videos, online ads and short documentaries. After many years of trying to forge a career from directing I turned my focus to writing longer pieces and working on my narrative writing skills. The CryoShed is the result of my self motivated education in writing fiction. There are more novels in the works.

I'm dyslexic and have encounted hard lessons and failure in chacing my goals but have now published a novel, something that only a few years ago I thought was completely out of my depth. I want encourage other young people but especially dyslexics to keep searching for something to be good at, especially when you've failed at many things in the past. Your talent will appear, but only if you look for it.

FOR MORE...

Sign up to get updates on The CryoShed and more of Sean's work through his website:
www.seanerobinson.com/about

Follow @seanerobinson on Instagram, @seanshouse on twitter and @sean.e.robinson on Tik Tok.

THE CRYOSHED INDEPENDANTLY PUBLISHED BY ELLAYE LTD

ellaye ltd

Printed in Great Britain
by Amazon

67622084R00119